THE
Magician's
TWITCH

Dear Mark and Ali,
Hope you enjoy
these latest adventures
of the Little People
Love and Blessings

Pastor old West

VOLUME TEN

THE

TWITCH

The Twith Logue Chronicles
Adventures with the Little People

KENNETH G. OLD
& PATTY OLD WEST

TATE PUBLISHING
AND ENTERPRISES, LLC

Published by Tate Publishing & Enterprises, LLC
127 E. Trade Center Terrace | Mustang, Oklahoma 73064 USA
1.888.361.9473 | www.tatepublishing.com

Tate Publishing is committed to excellence in the publishing industry. The company reflects the philosophy established by the founders, based on Psalm 68:11,
"The Lord gave the word and great was the company of those who published it."

Book design copyright © 2014 by Tate Publishing, LLC. All rights reserved.
Cover design by Rtor Maghuyop
Interior design by Caypeeline Casas
Poetry excerpts from Footprints in the Dust by Kenneth G. Old
Map design by Rich and Lisa Ballou

Published in the United States of America

ISBN: 978-1-62902-862-0
1. category:sub category
2. category: sub category
13.11.18

DEDICATION

Ken spinning tales of the Little People to children gathered on Sandes Hill

Dedicated to the children who first heard these
stories at the boarding school in Murree, Pakistan.

OTHER BOOKS BY KENNETH G. OLD

Walking the Way
Footprints in the Dust
A Boy and His Lunch
So Great a Cloud
Roses for a Stranger
The Wizard of Wozzle
Squidgy on the Brook
Gibbins Brook Farm
The Wizard Strikes Twice
Beyonders in Gyminge
The SnuggleWump Roars
The Secret Quest
Dayko's Rime
Circus in Sellindge

OTHER BOOKS BY PATTY OLD WEST

Good and Faithful Servant
Once Met, Never Forgotten
The Wizard of Wozzle
Squidgy on the Brook
Gibbins Brook Farm
The Wizard Strikes Twice
Beyonders in Gyminge
The SnuggleWump Roars
The Secret Quest
Dayko's Rime
Circus in Sellindge

To learn more about the books listed above, visit the
website: http://pattyoldwest.tateauthor. com

EAGLE'S FLIGHT

Better grasp at a flying star
Than seize the sweet fruit on the bough.
Better than walking tall, by far,
Is to soar with the eagles now.

~

When there is a chance to choose
There are things only birds can see.
Better by far wings than shoes.
Alas, earthbound mortals are we.

~

Better a child's mind set alight
With fantasy's call to be free
Than a hundred facts put right
To maintain its captivity.

ACKNOWLEDGMENTS

Ken Old was a man of many talents. The Lord endowed him with the ability to see beyond the every day and gave him the creative writing talent to put those dreams and visions onto paper. His unique way of looking at things opens up new vistas of imagination beyond the ordinary. It is my hope that while reading about the Little People, you can capture some of that same exciting, vibrant, carefree way of living and seeing.

Special thanks go to Margaret Spoelman, Patrick Wilburn, and Kim Dang for kindly making copies of the first chapters that Gumpa sent by e-mail. After being entered into the computer, Gumpa's creative genius generated more than would fit into one book. It was split and the two smaller stories were expanded once again. Those also became too large and had to be divided. Eventually, the initial few chapters became twelve volumes known as *The Twith Logue Chronicles*. They chronicle the adventures of the Little People as they are exiled from their homeland until they are able to return many centuries later.

It is with heartfelt gratitude and much appreciation that I acknowledge my darling daughters, Sandy Gaudette, Becky Shupe, and Karin Spanner. They were involved in every stage of editing from the initial shaping and refining of the text to the final proof reading. I also want to thank my professional editor, Germaine Canilao, who kindly commented that the story is entertaining, realistic, and engaging.

Finally, I must give credit to my dear, sweet, kind, considerate, thoughtful, and wonderful husband, Roy. At times, he must have felt like a widower once again as I spent so many hours with my nose pressed up against my computer screen. His patient, loving support has allowed me to continue the process of sharing these delightful stories with others.

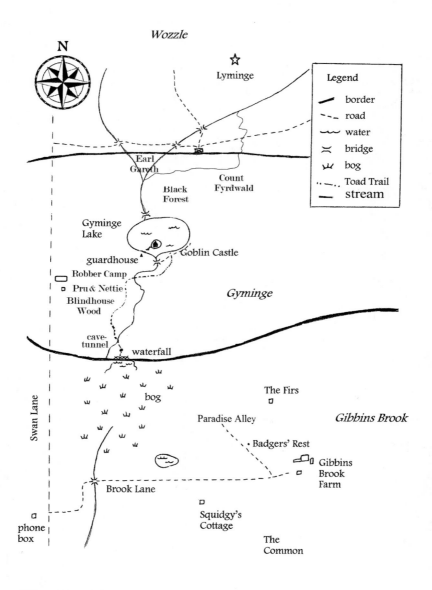

Wozzle and Gyminge, neighboring countries of Little People.
The Brook (or Common). Home for ten of the Little People.

Principal Characters

The Little People / Twith Logue
(TWI th LOW guh)

Jock	Leader of the Twith Logue
Jordy	Jock's roommate
Taymar	Jock's right-hand man
Ambro / Scayper	Taymar's brother
Gerald	Keeper of the Lore
Stumpy / Cleemo	Oldest of the Twith
Cymbeline (CYMBAL een)	Stumpy's niece
Barney	Stumpy's nephew, youngest of the Twith
Cydlo(SID low)	A woodcutter
Elisheba (Eh LISH eh buh)	His daughter
Dr. Vyruss Tyfuss	A new ally of the Twith

The Beyonders

Gumpa	An early friend of the Twith
Gran'ma	His wife
Bimbo and Bollin	Their married sons / Shadow children
Stormy	An American girl
Bajjer(BAD jur)	Her brother
Specs	An English boy
Ginger	His sister
Uncle Andy	Gumpa's brother

Sarah and Peter	Andy's oldest daughter and her husband
Mike and Vickie	Their children
Titch	Granddaughter from Texas
Katie and Gretchen	Sisters from Michigan
Rachael and Micah	Grandchildren from Washington
Austin and Lucas	Brothers from Washington
Jenn and Nick	Grandchildren from Idaho
Ruthie and Ellie	Shadow children
Penwith Nancarrow	Owner of a circus
Oolagoola	His Eskimo wife

THE BIRDS AND ANIMALS

Blackie	The leader of the rabbits
Buffo	The toad, doorkeeper for the Twith
Crusty	The eagle
Lupus	Cydlo's wolf-dog
Maggie	The magpie
Pia	Maggie's sister
Sparky	The sparrow
Tuwhit (Too WHIT)	The barn owl

THE WIZARD AND HIS CRONIES

Griswold (GRIZ walled)	The wizard
Rasputin (Rass PEW tin)	The wizard's raven
King Haymun	The king of the goblins
Jacko	The ferret
MoleKing / Moley	The king of the moles
Griselda Squidge / Squidgy	The old woman on the Brook
Cajjer(CAD jur)	Squidgy's cat
The SnuggleWump	Squidgy's watch-guard
The Teros	Titchy pterodactyls
Frijjilda / Frijji / Pansy	Squidgy's younger sister

PLACES

Gyminge (GIH minge)	Land of the Little People
Wozzle (WOZ el)	The kingdom of the wizard

DAYKO'S RIME

Forget not the land that you leave
As you flee from the pain and grief.
Let Truth in your heart ever burn.
It alone can bring your Return.

~

The hour the Return shall begin,
The captive shall tug at her chain.
Two spheres of night only you stay;
You shall not have longer a day.

~

From the water the shield will come,
The sword will come forth from the stone,
The dirk from the dust will return,
And the cloth will give up the crown.

~

The open door's better to guard
Than one which is bolted and barred.
Though conspire the foe and his friend
Yet the dog shall win in the end.

~

You go through the heart of the log,
Though the way is hid in the bog.
Black and white the flag high will rise.
The Child shall lead on to the Prize.

~

The goblet holds no draught of wine
And yields but a drop at a time.
The king will arise in the wood.
The Rime is at last understood.

The armour the flame will withstand.
Salt wind shall blow over the land
For light in the heart of the ring
Shall end the restraint of the king.

The belt is restored from the fire.
Brides shall process to the byre.
The loss of the Lore gives grief,
Though what is that to a life?

The fall will lead straight to the wall.
Hope is restored last of all.
Two reds in the night shall be green.
All's done. I've told what I've seen.

PREFACE

Gumpa loved to tell stories to children. It gave him a chance to be a child again himself. *The Twith Logue Chronicles*, which just means "Little People Stories," are fanciful, imaginative fairy tales that he told over a period of more than fifty years to children from ages five to fifteen. He just made them up as he went along, and the children always wanted to hear more. They would ask, "Will you please read some more out of your head?" When Gumpa retired, there weren't so many children around, so he began putting his thoughts into writing for children to read.

The stories are a mixture of reality and fantasy, and sometimes, it is hard to tell where one leaves off and the other begins. I think that sometimes he didn't even know himself. The reality part is the old Tudor farmhouse and the surrounding area known as Gibbins Brook in Kent, England. The fantasy part is the Little People who are only half a thumb high. The adventures they have with Gumpa are where reality fades into fantasy.

The villain in this story learned how to do magic as a boy and grew up to become a mean, nasty wizard. Because anyone who uses magic develops The Magician's Twitch, Griswold is plagued with a twitchy right eye. That has foiled the perfect execution of more than one superior plan conceived by his brilliant mind. The wizard is a master of deceit and illusion. One reason he can be so sly and sneaky is that he is a master of disguises and can change from one creature to another very quickly. He can change himself into *almost* anything as long as it moves and has an eye that can twitch.

The heroes of these stories are the Little People known as the Twith Logue or just plain Twith. They are far older than the English and have their origins in myth. These tiny folk are very wise and know many things we don't. They have senses we don't have so they can understand and talk to animals and birds. They do *not* use magic, and they *always tell the truth*. They know how to halt time, so they can stop growing older whenever they want. The youngest of them, Barney, has decided to stay a boy of ten. Even though they are only half a thumb high, they have managed to survive for many centuries. Winning battles doesn't always depend on how big you are. The Twith live in the east of England in the kingdoms of Gyminge and Wozzle, tiny lands just on the northern edge of Gibbins Brook and separated from it by a bog. The bog, along with the meadows and wooded common land surrounding it, is known locally as the Brook.

The wicked wizard learned about the Little People and felt they would know the cure for The Magician's Twitch. He decided to invade their countries and become their ruler. By the magic he learned a thousand years ago in Cornwall, he made himself small and conquered first Wozzle and then Gyminge. Many of the Little People refused to be his subjects, so he sealed them up in bottles and put them in the castle dungeons. The others he turned into goblins who serve in his army.

Seven of the Little People were able to escape with their valuable Book of Lore. It contains all the wisdom the Twith have acquired over the centuries. They could not return to Gyminge because of the invisible curtain that the wizard put around the land, so they settled on the Brook among the Beyonders. The people who live outside the land of the Little People are called Beyonders. The adults and children you know are all Beyonders. Very few Beyonders know about the Little People, so you are privileged to be learning about them.

Mrs. Squidge, an old woman from Cornwall, came to the Brook to ask the wizard's help with her magic. It sometimes goes wrong. Squidgy accidentally turned a lizard into a dragon-like creature with two long, sinuous necks that she calls a SnuggleWump. Each head has one eye in the center that changes from red to green depending on his mood. Later, her yeast buns changed six chickens into six tiny pterodactyls. That same batch transformed the king of the moles into a strange creature that the wizard calls a Zebrotter. He is actually a duck-billed platypus with zebra-like stripes. Squidgy became the wizard's main ally on the Brook, and he makes her cottage a base for his activities whenever he is there.

Now picture yourself sitting on Gumpa's knee or gathered with other children at his feet and listen as he puts you into the world of the Little People, challenging *you* to tell the truth and taking you into strange and exciting adventures.

PROLOGUE

The free Twith Logue who live on the Brook are counting the days they have left in the Beyond. Their ancient seer, Dayko, left them a Rime that indicates the events that must take place before they will be able to return to their homeland. Gerald, the newly appointed High Seer, has calculated the exact day when all those events must be completed. That date, August 12, is only six weeks away, and there are still many lines in the Rime that remain a mystery. Failure means they could possibly have to wait another thousand years for the next opportunity to return to Gyminge. They are determined, come-what-may, to return home this summer and restore their king to the throne. Then they will be able to release their friends and families the wizard has imprisoned in the dungeons at Goblin Castle.

For centuries, the wizard has been trying to capture the Twith who escaped so he can get hold of their Book of Lore. When Mrs. Squidge settled on the Brook, she met two of the Little People and told the wizard. Until then, he didn't know where to find those who had escaped. Now, he makes frequent excursions into the Beyond, attempting to capture them. On those occasions, he goes through a secret opening in the curtain. Once outside of Gyminge, he becomes a normal-sized man and changes back to Little People size when he returns.

The wizard has already made several attacks on the seven Little People. To begin with, he captured Stumpy, the oldest of the Twith. At the same time, their precious Shadow Book was stolen. The Shadow Book is something like a photograph album and contains the shadows of children who have helped the Twith in the past. Jock, the little Scottish leader of the Twith, collected their shadows, and Gerald, as Twith historian and record keeper, put them in the book. Both the book and Stumpy were successfully recovered, but with the wizard closing in, the Twith decided to enlist the help of Beyonder children. The children must *always tell the truth* or they will put the Little People in danger. The first four to arrive were Stormy and her brother, Bajjer, from America and Specs and his sister, Ginger, who are English. Children helping the Twith can become half a thumb high by holding the hand of one of the Little People. By crossing two fingers as the Little People hold their hand, the children resume their former stature. When the children are half a thumb high, they can understand and talk to animals and birds, but until then, they need an interpreter.

In an attempt to obtain the Book of Lore, the wizard changed himself into a dormouse. It was Stormy's gift to her brother for his birthday. Bajjer was successful in throwing him out of Twith Mansion. However, the Twith realized the wizard would attack again and sent for a dozen more children. Five Shadow children were also called to come help. Jock can call them back off the page, and they are the same age as when they helped so long ago. They are the same size as the Twith, but do not get hungry and are as light as butterflies.

The wizard does not accept defeat. He is determined to have that Book of Lore, so he craftily changed himself into a deliveryman. By tricking gran'ma into going outside with him, he captured her and took her to Goblin Castle. There, he chained her to the laundry room floor and put her to work ironing the uniforms of the goblin solders.

In over a thousand years, the Little People were never able to penetrate the invisible curtain around their homeland. But Buffo, the toad who acts as the Twith doorkeeper, showed them the way through a waterfall. Jock took half of his forces into Gyminge to rescue gran'ma. Crusty, the golden eagle, also found the way through by using the hole in the curtain that the wizard and his raven, Rasputin, use.

With Jock's forces split in two, the wizard made an all-out attack on the farmhouse. His secret weapon was Squidgy's SnuggleWump. The farm dog saw off the SnuggleWump, and the children were ready for the wizard and his other helpers. He was soundly defeated. At long last, the tide of struggle is changing. Things are no longer going all the wizard's way.

Gran'ma was rescued along with a woodsman, Cydlo, and his daughter, Elisheba. They are now part of the Twith family on the Brook.

Jock then sent Bimbo and Bollin, the two Shadow brothers, into Gyminge on a secret quest. When they returned, they brought with them the Royal Sword and the Royal Shield, thus fulfilling two more lines in Dayko's Rime. They also rescued Scayper, a prisoner they met when they were put in the most secure of the castle dungeons. Or so the wizard thought. There was actually a hidden escape door in that cell.

Many secrets were unveiled. To the amazement and joy of the Twith, Cydlo confessed that he is King Rufus, and his daughter Elisheba is Princess Alicia. Not only that, but in happier days long ago, she was betrothed by her father to the oldest son of the Earl of Up-Horton who is none other than Taymar, Jock's right-hand man.

Scayper surprised them twice. First, he revealed that he is Taymar's brother, Ambro. The other surprise was that Cymbeline, Stumpy's niece, is his long-lost love. Both couples plan to be married on the farm, so gran'ma is busy making preparations for a double wedding.

The wizard returned to Gyminge to investigate rumors of invisible Chinese invaders. He expected his troops to arrive from the Brook to help. When they failed to do so, and no invaders could be found, the wizard returned to Squidgy's cottage. He was scheming how to trick the Twith in order to finally gain possession of their Book of Lore. An opportunity presented itself with the arrival of a circus in the nearby village. He convinced the owner to bring the circus to the Brook. While the majority of his enemies were enjoying a special performance, he gained entry into Twith Mansion and stole the Book of Lore!

Now let's continue the mystery, the excitement, and the adventures of the Little People.

GOBLIN CASTLE

Griswold, the Wizard of Wozzle, returned from the Brook in the guise of a cormorant. On arrival home at his castle, he transformed back to himself and retired to his palatial apartment. After shaving and bathing, he allowed himself twice the usual amount of toothpaste—a customary signal of approval with himself. He enjoys the flavor and doesn't mind if he swallows a blob while brushing away. Now clothed in his pajamas, a dressing gown, and his slippers, he allows the court chiropodist to trim his toenails while the manicurist sees to his fingernails. His barber trims not only his thick, grey hair, but his bushy eyebrows and the hairs in his nose as well. Griswold believes in multi-tasking and expects his servants to perform likewise.

Now that his personal care is complete, the wizard settles down for a quiet afternoon alone in the lounge. He is relaxed and comfortable in his home setting. He turns his easy chair so that he has a view across the lake to the north shore. The ottoman serves as his footstool. On the side table is a bowl of fresh-plucked, dark-red cherries. He hums to himself and pops a couple of them into his mouth. Also on the table is a dish of his favorite mints and a tray with his afternoon tea—freshly made and piping hot. He only drinks Darjeeling. It is, after all, the champagne of teas.

He kicks off his slippers, looks for a moment or so at his toe-nails, and settles back for a long read. He has given notice that he is not to be disturbed until he rings the bell. He spits the cherry pips towards the fireplace. The tiny seeds miss the copper pot placed there by the servants in the vain hope the pips will fall in. The wizard reaches for a couple more cherries.

He is a man of medium height and spare frame, clean shaven, slightly stooped in the shoulders, just beyond middle age. His head is notable for a large, high forehead, a pair of very large ears, piercing dark brown eyes, a huge nose, and a broad, crooked mouth.

Griswold is absolutely elated with his prize. He picks up the Book of Lore from beside the tea tray and prepares to ferret out from his trophy the long sought for remedy for The Magician's Twitch. He is smugly satisfied. "It has been a good day! I have the Twith Book of Lore in my hands at last. I am going to enjoy the victor's spoils. Without my twitch, I will become invincible!" He likes that phrase and rolls it around his mind like the dregs in a teacup before a session of tealeaf reading.

"I feel like Alexander the Great after defeating the Persians at the Battle of Granicus or Wellington after defeating Napoleon at Waterloo." He sings to himself, making up nonsense rhymes where he is a valiant, brave hero. "Tra-la-la-la-la. Tra-la-la-la-lee!" He refocuses his thoughts. "Enough, Griswold, to the task at hand!"

With his long, bony fingers, he caresses the old, brown, vellum cover. He allows his thoughts to flicker over the day's brilliant achievements. *Yes, they were brilliant. No lesser adjective does justice to my achievements.* He looks with pleasure at the title inscribed on the cover in gold. He savors the sound as he reads it aloud. "*The Lore of the Twith Logue.*" He begins to laugh and almost chokes on a cherry pip, which slips from his mouth to his throat. Coughing it up, he spits it and the other pip towards the fireplace, once again missing the copper pot.

Reaching for two more cherries, Griswold wonders aloud, "Shall I start at the beginning? No, I can come back to that later. This afternoon is for relaxation and pleasure. The serious business of searching for the cure of the Magician's Twitch can wait a short while. I've waited a thousand or more years already. I'll dip in at random." The page he opens to is written in richly decorated, early medieval script that speaks of times long past. "This looks promising." As he makes himself comfortable, he smiles happily and hums the tune of an old Cornish nursery rhyme. He reads slowly, but as he reads, he stops humming.

His expression changes—and keeps changing. It grows darker and darker! "WHAT IS THIS?"

Cornish Pasty

Preheat oven to 400 degrees F.

Pastry
1 lb flour, 5 oz lard, pinch of salt, water to mix

Filling
1 lb best quality lean beef, 1 lb potatoes, 1 lb turnips, 1 small onion, 1 oz butter, pepper & salt to taste.

Make the pastry and divide into two equal pieces. Roll each piece into a round ten inches in diameter.

Finely slice the potatoes, parsnips, and onion. Cut the beef into small cubes, removing all fat. Place the potatoes on the pastry rounds, add the parsnips and onions. Then salt and pepper. Add the meat and a knob of butter and another sprinkle of pepper.

Dampen the edges of the pastry and bring up from both sides with floured hands to envelop the filling. Pinch the edges together and crimp them firmly to seal tightly.

Bake on a greased tray for 45 to 60 minutes.

Enjoy your meal!

The wizard's look, to put it gently, has soured. It has not only soured, it has curdled. He does not fault the recipe, although there are differences from the one used in the castle kitchen. It is more that he is suspicious. "I did not expect the inclusion of a pasty recipe in the Book of Lore! More than that, the ancient Lore of the Twith would have been written over a thousand years ago, and this is undoubtedly written in twentieth century terms." He is suddenly anxious.

He turns with rising disquiet to the beginning of the book. The first pages are filled with tips about the weather. "Red sky at night, sailor's delight. Red sky in morning, sailor's warning." There are age-old country clues to when spring arrives—dew, hawthorn berries, rosebuds, cuckoo bird calls—late or early—the dawn chorus, arrival of swallows, dandelion balls, bees and dragonflies, morning mist and evening fog, the direction of breezes, the prevalence or otherwise of gnats and butterflies, hoarfrost. "Now these are all in the old Twith idiom that I'm well acquainted with. I'm not surprised to find these in the Lore."

Next, however, come the recipes. And they keep on coming! He leafs through quickly with increasing haste. "The remainder of the entries in this book are recipes! There must be hundreds of them—how to make clotted cream, heavy cake, potato cake, saffron cake, splits, pot roast, ginger fairings, luncheon cake, pilchards, mutton and turnip pie, Cornish pasty, railway pudding, bacon and egg pie, yeast cake, starry gazey pie." The last few pages are still blank. "What about the wisdom of the Lore? Where's that?"

He slams the book down in disgust. "Almost the whole book, although written in medieval script, is a twentieth century recipe book for Cornish dishes! This is not the Twith Lore at all! I've been tricked! I risked my life and limb for this? All the brilliance of my immaculate planning and execution are gone to waste!

"How dare they! I'll make them pay for this! The gloves are off now. If they want warfare, they can have warfare! This is plain deceit, it's just not cricket. Even a cad of the most cunning nature would not do this. Aren't the Twith supposed to stick to the truth? Isn't that what they boast about? Undoubtedly, they are laughing at me right now. Me! The Wizard of Wozzle—the world's greatest master of disguise, a world class leader, a brilliant thinker! How dare they laugh at me!

"Well, they've got another think coming. I'll knock those silly laughs right off their faces!"

GRISWOLD RALLIES

The thwarted magician considers what he might throw. He holds back his instinct to pitch the useless book through the window. "Rain looks likely, and it's coming from the north. It could blow in through a smashed window." He looks at the tea tray holding fine antique china. He is tempted to throw the whole lot, but refrains from doing so. "That will be difficult to replace." Finally, his eyes fall on the bowl of cherries. By firm self-control, he limits himself to spitting, in quick succession, the two cherry pips in his mouth as far towards the fireplace as he can. Both fly further than he has ever reached before, exploding into the quiet space beyond the copper pot.

He admonishes himself. "Steady, Griswold, steady. Remember, you are a leader! Remember Agincourt! Remember Thermopylae. Remember the Battle of the Nile." He draws a deep breath and tells himself, "Maintain self-control, Griswold! Draw on your reserves. Remember your mottoes, my good fellow. Desperate times, my lad, call for desperate remedies. Think, lad, think. Which motto?" *Who dares, wins*? "No good that one. I have dared brilliantly…and lost." *Deceive, divide, conquer*? "That's no good either. The Twith have deceived me instead." *The early bird catches the worm*? "A fat lot of good staying up all night has done!" *Every failure is an opportunity in disguise*? "Yes! That will have to do."

Griswold moans, "I have failed when I thought I had succeeded." He straightens himself up and squares his shoulders. "Don't wallow in self-pity, man. Think, Griswold, think! Focus! How do I turn this failure into an opportunity?" He concentrates and puts himself back onto the Brook, into the farmhouse this morning, down the narrow, twisting staircase into Twith

Mansion, and into the silent passageway. *Was it only this morning this all happened?*

He is once more in the corridor of Twith Mansion, hiding behind the curtain, leaning forward, listening. *What are the two in the dining room saying? I don't recognize the man's voice. But it must be the red-haired man with a limp. The boy with the spectacles just called him Cydlo. Somehow, that rings a chord. Now, what did he say exactly?*

"This is important, Specs. The first thing we must do is check what we have against Dayko's original Rime. There's no need to wait for Gerald to get back from the circus. He left me his keys. They are hidden in my room. I know where he keeps the Rime, inside the cover of the Book of Lore. He has been working hard on that lately, and it may well be in his desk drawer either in the office or the records room. Let's go see."

That was when I spotted the salt and pepper shakers I used later to create a distraction. I heard again, less clearly, that same man's voice from beyond the open door.

"We're lucky, Specs. Gerald has been working on the Lore, it's here. And here is the Rime, inside the cover. Now, let's take a look at verse seven. There, look. Line two doesn't have a full stop. What can that possibly mean?"

He grins as he remembers, *I immediately sprung into action and was in total control of the rapid sequence of events that left my enemies shattered. I quickly gained possession of the Book of Lore. Transforming myself into Skullbones, the pirate boy, I made my escape with my loot in hand right through the front door of the farmhouse in broad daylight, totally unobserved.* He laughs with amusement and then grows sober.

He mutters to himself, "The first thing I need to do now is to look at my own copy of Dayko's Rime. Squidgy's sister cleverly obtained it for me on her visit to the farmhouse disguised as a schoolgirl." He is no longer in the mood for cherries and pushes the bowl aside. It falls off the edge of the table and smashes. He ignores it. "What are servants for?" He fishes around in his pockets, finds the paper, and smoothes it out flat on the table. Picking it back up, he scans the poem. "The verse they were talking about was verse seven. Here it is."

> *The armour the flame will withstand.*
> *Salt wind shall blow over the land*
> *For light in the heart of the ring*
> *Shall end the restraint of the King.*

"The pair of them were only concerned about the second line and the fact that it didn't have a full stop. What that means is that line two leads into line three without a pause. What ring is Dayko talking about? What is it the boy noticed?"

Suddenly, he understands. It is glaringly obvious, clear as daylight. Like a sunbeam into a cellar! "The red-headed man with the limp is not only Cydlo, he is King Rufus! Here I thought he had died in the Beyond, but he is still alive! After all these centuries, the old enemy has reemerged. The red hair fits. His limp means he must have been wounded in the leg as well as in the chest in the battle at Fowler's Bridge those many centuries ago."

With a connecting flash of genius that separates the men from the boys, the wizard puts his anger and disappointment behind him. His mind works like lightning as he readjusts his thinking. "So, King Rufus is back in the picture. That may well make the enemy weaker than stronger. The king brings with him weak links that can be exploited." He laughs uproariously. "I am ahead of the enemy again. They do not know that I know, and that is a clear advantage!"

A germ of an idea begins to sprout in the dark recesses of the wizard's mind. A split-second is all that is needed to turn a failure into an opportunity. His mouth twists into a sinister sneer. "I have at my disposal information no one else knows that will be of great interest to the king. I will force him to his knees in surrender."

He leans back, takes a long, deep breath, pours himself another cup of tea, adds an extra spoonful of sugar, and rings the bell for another bowl of cherries and a fresh pot of tea.

Griswold allows himself a hint of a smile. "Suddenly, the sun has emerged from behind thunder clouds. Opportunity rather than failure is knocking, and knocking loud and clear." Another motto springs to mind. *Who dares, wins!* He sneers menacingly. "Griswold, the supreme leader, is marshaling his forces once again! The struggle is by no means over. In fact, it is entering an entirely new phase and is only just beginning!"

THE SUMMONS

It is late afternoon in Gyminge. At the southern border, along the edge of the bog, all is quiet. The mother toads are all back on the Brook with their young. There is no one coming or going through the tunnel to disturb the guards who sleep most of the time.

Colonel Tyfuss, Commander of the Southern Zone, is almost happy. Sometimes, he sings to himself. He is proud of his tenor voice, and he sings in his bath with gusto. This excites the toads across the border in the Beyond, and they join in with their own unique accompaniment.

He is in the prime of life, relatively young, and not too bad looking. Apart from his flat feet, he has no major ailments. He no longer regrets being relieved of his duties as chief medical officer of the castle and personal physician to the goblin king. He has been put in charge of constructing the immigration control center near the cave-tunnel at the southern border. He is half a kingdom away from the castle and the interference of the king and the wizard. Their presence can be guaranteed to be unsettling. The further away they are, the better for everybody. The colonel is beginning to enjoy his promotion to a position where he can exercise authority. He is his own boss and has learned how to pass orders down the line of command. Eventually, when there is nowhere lower for the orders to go, they stop moving and things begin to happen.

He has adequate troops under his command and work is proceeding steadily. The king continues to supply the sketches that provide the drawings and details for building the border fort. Colonel Tyfuss makes no effort to understand them. He passes them on down the line to Major Bubblewick. The official residences for dignitaries are the top priority. The king has been thinking of himself and making sure the buildings and the furnishings are of the highest standard. Each evening, there is an inspection of the work by the colonel and his ring of subordinates. They help him write a report on progress for the day that is sent by the mounted messenger returning with mail to the castle.

Behind the colonel's own large tent is one of the largest colonies of woodlice in the whole kingdom. Vyruss has always been fascinated with these little creatures. Often, while others might think he is working in his office, he is on his knees out back, watching and making notes of the way the woodlouse leaders give orders, deal with mutiny and disobedience, and organize their labor gangs. He is amused. "Although they appear to be highly organized and extremely busy, they are achieving nothing. What a superb model for higher forms of life such as the army. The dignity of labor is preserved without the pressure of any progress needing to be achieved." He lifts his head as he hears approaching hoof beats. Glancing at his watch, he thinks, *It must be the mail messenger. I better return to my office.*

As he strolls across to his tent, he is thoughtful. Up until recently, woodlice have been his main interest. However, his short stay on the Brook with the free Twith has altered his thinking about a lot of things. For one, he cannot get out of his mind the beautiful young Cymbeline. Vyruss admits to himself, *I would rather be watching her. She has such a sweet and ready smile. Her face glows with an inner light when she smiles. I remember how her brown eyes twinkle and that bit of a tilt to her nose. Her glossy brown hair falls so lightly on her shoulders and curls up at the ends. She has such tiny hands with lovely, slender fingers.* He sighs, "Aah!"

Settling himself at his desk, he calls for the orderly and orders tea. He smiles with pleasure. *Her name is music to my ears.* He voices it aloud. "Cymbeline." He smiles and repeats it a tone higher. "Cymbeline." He feels a poem coming on. *I wonder what rhymes with Cymbeline?* He can't think of a word and puts the poem aside. *I wonder how she would react to a military mustache, waxed to a point at both ends?* He twitches his upper lip once or twice, and thinks, *I'll make up a false one from cotton wool and try it out before I shave again. If I do decide to grow one, there's no time like the present to start.* The orderly brings tea and Vyruss is jolted back to reality.

The daily messenger from the castle has arrived. His horse is being fed and watered. The mail he brought is spread out on a table for sorting. This is the most important event of each day. Once the mail arrives in camp, all work ceases until the mail is sorted, delivered, and perused.

Vyruss settles down to read the latest batch of mail from the castle. The large brown envelope with King Haymun's familiar handwriting he puts aside. There are a number of general letters relating to the matters of the garrison under his management. These are easily recognized without opening, and those he also sets aside. With great unease, he recognizes the handwriting on the only letter left. It is the Commander-in-Chief's own distinctive scribble that looks as though a spider seized an ink-dipped worm and dragged it, protesting and wriggling, across the front of the envelope. This can mean only one thing, *Trouble!* It says simply:

Colonel Tyfuss
Urgent & Personal

Dropping the envelope back on the tray, Vyruss adds more sugar to his tea, stirs vigorously, and gulps it down as though this will sustain him for what lies ahead. Nervously, he twitches his upper lip as though he already has a mustache. *What has the wizard found out about me? Can I escape back to the Brook before they cart me off in chains to the castle dungeons? Has the wizard's magic told him that he has a traitor in his midst? Does he know that one of his men is a turncoat, determined against all military standards and principles, to only speak the truth? Has he discovered that one of his men, one of his trusted lieutenants, even worse, a colonel no less, is betraying the cause? Boiling in oil would be a light punishment to mete out to such a villain. More likely, it will be boiling in vinegar!* Vyruss has never liked vinegar and doesn't understand why people use it. He grimaces.

He draws a deep breath and pulls himself together. "What would a woodlouse do in such circumstances? No, it's no good going down that road. Only a few days ago, I almost drowned in the bog because of using that line of thinking.

"Open the letter, Vyruss," he says to himself as though giving an order to a reluctant goblin on the carpet for failing to salute. He looks around to make sure no one is looking on to observe his nervousness, licks the butter knife clean, and uses it to slit the envelope open. The handwritten note is a short one—terse, ominous, and undated.

> *Colonel Tyfuss, You are reassigned effective immediately. Hand over your duties to your next in command and return here to arrive no later than noon tomorrow. Report immediately to me.*

The note is signed with the characteristic squiggle that allows no doubt as to its author.

Vyruss needs to move quickly. The cavalryman who brought the mail is told not to depart without further orders. They will travel in company. The colonel's personal servant is young. This is his first spell of duty away from home, and he has just received in the mail a brush-off from his girlfriend. Dudley sits behind the colonel's tent, sobbing silently. When he is sent for, he brushes his tears away. *I hope no one notices. If they do, I'll explain it's due to an allergy to woodlouses.* He hasn't been happy with his assignment. *I didn't join the army to be a nursemaid to a bunch of woodlouses! I hate woodlouses! I'm tempted to kick their habitations to kingdom come.* But he holds back. *I'm afraid I'd end up in the castle dungeons.*

Vyruss tells the lad, "Go pack up all my belongings. Be quick about it. I'll be leaving shortly."

Dudley wonders if that includes the woodlouses, but he doesn't have time to gather them up and put them in shipping boxes.

Vyruss writes the daily progress report for the king without the help of his regular subordinates. He sends for Major Bubblewick who oversees construction. "I have been ordered back to the castle. You will be in charge until my return. I'm sure you will manage very well without me."

The major salutes smartly. "Yes, sir." He is an army officer through and through. He knows that the most important thing to ensure that his career continues to improve is to make sure the colonel has good memories of the farewell he received. He needs all the friends in higher places he can gather.

Vyruss pops out to say good-bye to his woodlouses and make a few final observations.

Major Bubblewick gives quick instructions to his men. Soon, trumpets are sounding from one end of the camp to the other. Soldiers stuff away their letters from home and scour the hedges for flowers that can make farewell bouquets. Dungarees are exchanged for dress uniforms. The best of the garrison's three horses is polished and brushed till it glistens like a racehorse. The second best is loaded with the colonel's belongings and mounted by his personal servant who has claimed compassionate leave because of the death of both grandmothers in a boating accident. Dudley neglects to mention that it happened when he was a babe in arms.

Colonel Tyfuss will soon be on his way north.

THE SURPRISE
ASSIGNMENT

At Goblin Castle, the wizard wastes no time dwelling on his disappointment at being tricked with a pseudo Book of Lore. He is resolute and determined. "The way ahead is clear. Focus, Griswold, on the future. Not the past. This time there is to be no battle between massed forces. This time it will be hand-to-hand combat between two champions—Griswold versus King Rufus. And I am choosing both the weapons and the battlefield. It is Goliath versus David, and I am Goliath! Let there be no doubt about it! Things are going to be sorted out once and for all!"

King Haymun was informed that, for reasons of State, he is to stay out of the way this morning. The wizard has no plans to let him have any part in this latest move. "The man is an imbecile and likely to try to improve on the perfect. In addition to that, he is accident prone."

First, Griswold sets the stage. Servants are bustling to and fro in the formal sitting room where events are planned to take place. The ornaments are spotless, dusting is complete. The windows shine, and the chandeliers sparkle. The last fly has been hunted down and dispatched. Even the tiniest spiders are in hiding, trembling with fear. They themselves have destroyed any webs the servants did not discover lest the next purge be worse than the last.

A long, low table is brought and placed in front of the fireplace. A decorated tablecloth is laid on it. It is summer, no fire is needed, and the fireplace is empty of all save the fire tongs and grate. A large heavy tapestry cloth is folded over the back of one of the two chairs nearby. On a small side table, inconspicuously placed, are a basin and water ewer, soap and washcloths, small personal face towels, a hand mirror, brush, and comb.

Instead of a large dining table, a small circular table is placed near the fireplace. Three places are set using the best fine china, silverware, and crystal water goblets. Vases of flowers are brought in and placed on the serving tables, windowsills, and mantelpiece. A single red rose, barely more than a large bud, adorns the small dining table.

At the corner window, a writing table is placed in the alcove to benefit from the view over the lake. It contains the necessary supplies for writing letters—pen and ink, paper and envelopes, a bottle of drying sand, sealing wax, an unlit candle, and the castle seal. A dainty vase with another single rose sits on the far edge.

In the guest apartments of the north wing, two suites of rooms are being readied for use by guests. The wizard inspects both, checking particularly the door and the window. In each room, the window is merely a narrow slit suitable for an archer to fire an arrow through. The wizard is satisfied with the preparations. He checks the attire of the deaf and dumb servant girl who will attend to the wants of the guests in their rooms. In one of the rooms is an array of neatly stacked wooden boxes brought out of storage and dusted till they are spotless. Some of the contents now hang on hangers in the wardrobe.

In the kitchen, early preparations for the meal are underway. No time has yet been given for the meal. The wizard looks up at the clock above the entrance door. It is five minutes to noon. *The colonel only has five more minutes to make his entrance.* He has no need to concern himself. There is a knock. The last servant in the room, checking that all the arrangements satisfy the host, answers the door at the wizard's nod.

Colonel Tyfuss stands at attention. "Reporting for instructions, sir."

The wizard goes across to welcome the arrival and dismisses the one remaining servant with a nod of his head. He has been given his instructions earlier. The servant returns promptly with a tray of tea and hazelnut biscuits. He sets it down and then leaves the room and does not return.

Vyruss has spent eight hours in the saddle with only one break on the way in Blindhouse Wood for a few hours of restless sleep. He is tired and sore and dusty, to say nothing of being hungry and thirsty. He is not accustomed to such long journeys on horse-back. He hoped to have a rest before reporting to the wizard, but it has not been possible.

Only a week ago, the ex-doctor exercised his mind with frantic thoughts of doom when he was being pursued through the forest by King Haymun armed with a sharpened carving knife. That desperate run to save his life was a quiet jog in the woods amongst the primroses and foxgloves compared with this journey to the castle. His mind has been full of terrible thoughts anticipating being hung, drawn, and quartered or being burned at the stake. Even worse, he could be flogged to within an inch of his life and then tied down and subjected to Chinese water torture for the rest of his days using vinegar instead of water.

He is caught by surprise at his reception. There is no anger, no storm of rage, no abuse, no jumping up and down. Instead, he is being welcomed like a valued guest and treated to a cup of tea and hazelnut biscuits.

The wizard is solicitous. "Have you had a good journey? Fortunately, the weather has been fine. I regret the short notice, but I'm sure you have left the southern border in good hands. An urgent matter of State has arisen that calls for superior skills of diplomacy and sensitivity. To my knowledge, there is only one man available in the entire kingdom with an outstanding measure of these qualities. You, my good doctor, came immediately to mind. I want to ask you, as a personal favor, whether you would be willing to volunteer for reassignment as Ambassador of Gyminge to the Beyond for an indefinite length of time. I know that is a foreign country to you, but it will offer an opportunity to extend your experience abroad. And it will look well on your records."

Vyruss is confused. The dominant emotion in his confusion is gratitude. *It is apparent that the wizard has no awareness of my brief excursion through the waterfall and my near drowning in the bog. That information is better not shared, and I hope that King Haymun was wise enough to work that out also.* He heaves a sigh of relief. *I'm not going to be strung up by my thumbs and beaten with a thousand lashes by the two strongest men in the land after all! I would have been willing to volunteer for anything to avoid such treatment. This makes the decision easy.*

He is inclined to snap to attention, click his heels together smartly, and snap out, "Aye, aye, sir," in imitation of his own sub-ordinates. *I wonder whether that is the right reaction for an ambassador-in-waiting?* He contents himself with, "Yes, sir. I would be honored to serve in whatever capacity you desire." He recognizes with a certain regret, *I'll be losing the red tabs on my lapels. They give a certain aura of power. No doubt, there will be other compensations, though.* Floating back into his mind is another thought. *Perhaps I'll be seeing the delightful Cymbeline once again. It will give us an opportunity to refresh and strengthen our acquaintance. She gave me such a sweet parting smile as I left.* He doesn't know that the smile was not intended for him, but for Bimbo and Bollin, the two Shadow brothers.

"Perhaps," he begins with due deference, "you would be good enough, sir, to outline for me the duties you have in mind."

The wizard leans forward towards him and speaks more softly. "It is essential for reasons of State, my dear Colonel Tyfuss, that Gyminge obtains the Twith Book of Lore that is currently located at Gibbins Brook Farm in the Beyond. It is not far from our southern boundary. That is the hideout for the Gang of Seven, the Twith rebels that have been causing our country so much expense and trouble. They are assisted by a number of interfering

Beyonders that they have gathered on their side. I intend to also teach them a lesson in due course.

"I have just discovered that King Rufus, the old king of Gyminge who I defeated, is there in Twith Mansion. Possibly you remember him. I am, as you know, a man of peace. To avoid further conflict, I am about to make him a proposal that will be for our mutual benefit and the peace of our country. You, my dear Dr. Tyfuss, are going to be the negotiating intermediary between us. This will require not only high skill on your part, but a total change in your thinking about our country's best interests. You will have to put to the back of your mind all your valuable past experience in the service of Gyminge.

"Our national policy is that the causes of the nation come first and they are rarely served by truthfulness. However, the present circumstances are unusual. We will outwit the enemy and turn the tables on them by using truth as our weapon against them. Even though it will be severely limiting, I expect you to speak and tell *only* the truth. Do you think you can manage to do that?"

Vyruss breathes a sigh of relief. *I've already promised the Twith I would make the attempt to do just that.* He restrains himself from smiling and maintains a serious expression as he nods his head slightly.

The wizard thought the sigh was one of unease and uncertainty. He is pleased to see the nod of agreement. "Good. Undoubtedly, this will be very difficult, but not impossible for a man of your vast capacity and mental agility. However, I must warn you to be very alert. I believe that the rebels have some secret detector device that enables them to know whether what they are being told is truth or falsehood. I recall such a device I saw once in my youth.

"To obtain and hold their trust, you must tell the truth and only the truth at all times whenever you are in contact with them. In order to assist you, I have deliberately arranged matters so that there will be no need for you to do anything but tell the truth about everything you see and hear from now on. You will not be told any lies. There will be no need for you to decorate any story to make it more believable. What is now about to happen here in this room, you may talk about to the enemy quite openly.

"To succeed in your task, you need to persuade the Twith that you are open and honest and that you have complete integrity. That obviously represents a great challenge, but I have every confidence in you. I do not think there is a better man in the whole of Gyminge to achieve this transformation than yourself. Your success in this assignment is critical to the achievement of my future plans. I'm depending on you, Mr. Ambassador, to persuade the king to agree to my proposal. Don't disappoint me."

THE FLAG AND THE PLAN

The wizard is quite pleased with his new strategy. He chuckles delightedly. "Using the truth as a weapon will throw the Twith totally off guard."

He explains to Vyruss. "So far, we are right on schedule, but we need to move along if you are to get underway by tomorrow morning. There are quite a few details to take care of before lunch."

The colonel is sorry to hear that. He fears his stomach will soon start to growl with hunger pains. He keeps a stiff upper lip and says nothing.

The wizard goes silent. His brain is mult-itasking. *It is not yet time to send orders for delivery of the meal. I have to give Rasputin his instructions. I must write a letter to Mrs. Squidge explaining how I was unable to return to the cottage once the circus was over. But those things can wait until a bit later.*

He holds his hands out before him with the thumbs bent back and fingers outspread. Wiggling his fingers, he thinks, *This is why I am so effective. I'm a puppet master pulling all the strings.* He waggles his elbows like wings as though he has two additional strings attached to them. Fingers, thumbs, and elbows all waggle simultaneously. They are perfectly coordinated, not a movement unplanned for or out of correct timing. *My foes on the Brook will respond to my every tug on their strings, totally unaware that they are actually dancing to my tune.* He laughs out loud. *Poor David, he doesn't stand a chance! He is up against a Goliath with brains!*

The wizard remembers his guest who watches him with a confused look on his face. "You look like you could use some nourishment. I'll ring the bell for some cherries."

A servant scurries in.

Griswold inquires, "Is the flag ready?"

The servant nods, but before he can reply, the wizard says, "Then bring it in! And bring a large bowl of cherries. Be sure they are the dark-red ones."

The servant returns with the bowl of cherries and one of the Gyminge flags used by the lancers when they are on parade. On the long, thin, pointed pole is a black flag similar to the one now flying over the castle. However, there is one striking difference to the usual lancer flag. A large white circle is sewn on each side of the black flag so that there is only a narrow black border at top and bottom. The side borders are wider.

The wizard examines it closely and nods his head. He is satisfied with the sewing. "Yes, this looks fine."

The servant places the flag against the wall near the door as he leaves.

Griswold turns to Vyruss. "You must remember everything you see and hear from now on. We will have a guest joining us for lunch whom you have never met. King Haymun is unfortunately indisposed or there would be four of us. We shall also enjoy dinner together at seven o'clock, and then it will be early to bed for us. I will allow you to have a full night's rest before you embark on your new role as Ambassador of Gyminge to the Beyond." He smiles genially at his new ambassador whose mind is reeling with the thought of needing to remember everything he hears or sees for the entire rest of the day.

The wizard outlines the plans he has for Vyruss regarding his new assignment. "We must discuss your travel arrangements, explain about the flag, and the details of the proposal I have for the king. I will send you off south with the mail messenger tomorrow morning. Before you leave after breakfast, I shall give you two, possibly three, letters for King Rufus. One I shall allow you to read, and I will respond to any questions you might have before I sign and seal it. When you travel south, the mail messenger can carry the flag. You will proceed to the border and wait until nightfall. As darkness falls, my raven, Rasputin, will arrive. He will give you any further instructions from me. Then try and get some rest.

"An hour and a half before dawn, send out a dozen men with lamps to fully light the cave-tunnel from one end to the other. It is to be kept fully lighted until you have returned to this country and we have the Book of Lore safely in our hands. One hour before dawn, no later, you and Rasputin will both proceed through the toad tunnel to the Brook beyond. Take no weapons with you, only the letters and the flag. With the cave-tunnel brightly lit, Rasputin can lead the way. He does not enjoy that part of the journey. He was once severely burned going through there, so tell the men to be careful with the lamps. You have not been that way before so go carefully. The roof of the tunnel dips at about half distance and can catch the unwary a severe blow." Remembering his own misadventures, he reaches up and rubs his head thoughtfully. "Don't, whatever else you do, hit your head on the roof or you will have difficulty."

Vyruss wonders, *How did I manage the first time? I must have been running with my head down for faster speed.*

The wizard continues, "When you reach the waterfall, you will climb down a path to your right to the level of the bog. As soon as you are through the waterfall and the curtain beyond it, Rasputin will enlarge to Beyonder-size. Pause a moment or so to allow him to adjust, and then follow him onto the bog. Have no fear. I will instruct him well. He will pick you up in his claws before your feet are even wet and carry you to your destination. He has performed this service for King Haymun on occasion. It will be mere routine for him and smooth sailing for you. He will drop you as close to the enemy as possible where it is safe for him to do so. I am sure you will find your first flight by bird an exciting experience that will suit your spirit of adventure and give you a taste for many more similar journeys."

Vyruss adds no words of correction. *Truthfulness does not necessarily include correcting your boss when he is wrong. I have already had two eagle flights, but I'm keeping that to myself.*

The wizard moves ahead with his instructions. "From then on, you will be on your own. Listen carefully now. Everything depends on you. I have good reason to believe that the rebels expect a messenger with a black-and-white flag. You may be a stranger to them, but the flag you carry will be your authority. It is not a surrender flag—that would be all white. This is a negotiating flag. Raise your flag high above your head as soon as you see one of the Twith or anyone standing guard duty. Call out loudly, 'Peace! Peace! I come in peace!' They will not question your arrival.

"When you are taken before their leader, do not be afraid. There is only a small number of them. Explain you are the Ambassador of Gyminge to the Beyond. I have put credentials in this small envelope which show that I have properly appointed you and you are acting under my authority. Inform them that you have a message from me that is for the king and can only be handed directly to him.

"If they should deny that the king is present, simply state that you cannot deliver your message and need to return to Gyminge without delay. They will soon find the king for you. Tell them that I am expecting you safely back at the waterfall by noon on Wednesday at the latest. Should you be delayed, I will assume you are being held captive and will act accordingly.

"When you go before the king, first give him the credentials showing you have been authorized to act on my behalf. He must approve those before you can proceed. Then, simply offer him the letter that our guest at lunch will undoubtedly be writing to him. That one will be a private letter. Neither you nor I need to know its contents, and we shall make no attempt to find out. Simply ensure that it gets put into his hands safely."

The wizard smirks. "It is our secret weapon. The king may choose to leave and read his letter privately. Wait until he is ready, and then present my letter containing the proposal for him to consider. There may or may not be others present. It matters not. Inform him I suggested that you read the message aloud. I shall explain the details to you before you leave. When you finish reading it, ask if he has any questions. Answer all that you are able to, and be truthful. They will be watching you carefully and they need to trust, not me, but you, in order for us to proceed in the right direction. Do you have any questions thus far?"

Vyruss wonders, *Does asking questions to which I already know the answer constitute a lie?* He decides it does not, but to play safe, he merely answers, "I will wait until you reveal the complete plan that you have in mind. I'll save my questions until just before I leave."

The wizard leaps to his feet. "Then, Colonel, let us meet our guest."

THE LUNCH GUEST

The wizard gives strict orders to his servants. "You are to remain outside until I send for you. No one, no matter how important, is to enter until permission is given. Understood?"

Heads nod in agreement.

The wizard removes the heavy tapestry cloth on the back of the chair and places it on the long, low table in front of the fireplace. He also covers as much of the floor around the table as he can. Remaining on the chair is a white dusting cloth. The wizard has thought of everything. Satisfied with this arrangement, he smiles at his mystified guest. Before he proceeds any further, he turns to explain, "I consider it better that the servants know as little as possible about what I am going to show you. These days, you just don't know who you can trust.

"You will recall that during the drought, the lake was deepened and extended all around the castle. During the excavations, we discovered an underwater tunnel built of stone leading south from the castle to the east quarry. We demolished the portion that was in the lake and used the stones to enlarge the castle. We checked all around the castle lest there be other undiscovered tunnels, but we found none. In the part of the tunnel within the castle, there was a hidden room behind this fireplace and then a flight of steps down into the long tunnel to the outside.

"At the first landing beyond the hidden room, we blocked off the flight of steps so that there could never be any use of the tunnel to disturb the peace of the realm. There is no way anyone getting into the tunnel from the lake can make their way on into the castle. I have kept this secret fireplace room available for my private use and prefer that you make no reference of it to anyone. Not even King Haymun knows about it. Some things are better kept secret, even from friends. However, you may certainly mention it to King Rufus when it is appropriate. He will be well aware of its existence. Let me show you the room and where the blocking was done."

They step around the table and go forward to stand in front of the fireplace. Griswold pushes the fire grate and tongs to one side with his foot. Vyruss is puzzled as he watches the wizard, standing on tiptoe, trying to reach something behind one of the stones that support the thick timber mantelpiece. With great effort, he catches hold of something that Vyruss cannot see. As he pulls with his hand, one whole side of the inner part of the fireplace swings open almost noiselessly. The stone pivots bear and balance on oiled oak beams at the top and bottom.

Vyruss can see into a small room that is sparsely furnished. It has no light other than what comes from the room where they stand. A low arched opening at the far side is blocked with more recent masonry. That is where the flight of stairs once allowed exit to the outside. The wizard points out a tiny spy-hole that looks back into the room when the door is closed.

However, Vyruss isn't much interested in that. What catches his attention is a pair of trestles upon which rests something like a coffin covered with a plain green cloth. It has been there a long time for it is heavily layered with dust.

Griswold nods towards it. "Come, Colonel, I think we can manage this between us. You take this end and I'll take the other end. We'll carry it over to the table I just prepared for it and see what it is. Avoid disturbing the dust if you can."

Even before Vyruss steps into the secret room and lifts, he has worked out what the covered object is. Its size betrays what it is. It is one of the green-tinted glass bottles in which the wizard keeps his captives. He has seen only a few of them, but he has certainly heard a lot about them.

A chill of fear courses through him. *Is this the end for me? Has all of this good nature been one of the wizard's charades leading up to*

*an imminent call to the servants to return and slip this guest perma-
nently into storage? I just hope it will not be too cold. I prefer summer
to winter. It will be horrible to be a captive in a block of ice trying to
keep an active mind exercised. It will be like a lively goldfish in a bowl
of water suddenly frozen or turned into a strawberry popsicle.*

Vyruss shudders. *Everything is suddenly terribly obvious. This is
what lies behind my summons to the castle. The wizard knows all about
my secret pact with Jock and the other Twith. He has just been playing
with me as an angler plays a fish until he tires of the amusement.*

He lifts his end, and as he does, in an instant, hope is restored
and comes flooding back in. He sighs and smiles. The wizard, not
knowing his desperate thoughts, smiles back. *I can tell from the
feel that I'm right about what it is. It is a bottle. I have the bottom end
of it. But the bottle is not empty! It is heavy. There is someone already
in it.* He could almost break out singing, but he will save that
for bath time. *Perhaps everything is going to be all right after all.*
Uncertainly, he walks backwards, holding his end to keep it level.

The wizard guides him. "Be careful. Lift your right foot up
so you don't trip on the carpet. Easy now. Another step and you
need to step up onto the tapestry." Between them, they lower,
slide, and accurately position the cloth-covered bottle until it is
lying centered on the table. Griswold nods his approval.

Together, being careful not to create a cloud of dust, they roll
up the cover cloth from the bottom. The wizard instructs Vyruss,
"Return the cloth to the hideaway room. Be sure you don't spill
any dust on the carpets." Meanwhile, he busies himself wiping
the bottle clean.

The colonel is curious. The greenish tint to the misty glass
obscures the contents. *I wonder who it will be that emerges? Surely,
this must be the guest the wizard said would be joining us for lunch.
It will clearly be someone that King Rufus knows. Can it be Taymar's
younger brother or maybe even his father? Taymar questioned me
about both of them.*

He will soon find out. Clearly, there is someone inside, but there are no signs of movement. The wizard is on his knees using the poker to lever off the layer of candle wax that seals the plug in the top of the bottle. It does not prove to be a problem and peels away easily. All the loose wax is placed into the dusting cloth. The wizard clears the wax away from two pull handles. This particular wooden stopper is designed for ease of removal. At last, he is satisfied.

It is time for a good pull by both men. Griswold pulls on the stopper handles while Vyruss holds on tight to the rectangular base of the bottle and pulls in the other direction. His hands are close to slipping off, but the wizard smiles and nods his head. "The stopper is moving!"

Vyruss knows what to do next. He hurries around and holds the dusting cloth to catch both the stopper and the little fragments of remaining wax moving with it. He wraps the cloth tightly around its contents so they will not spill and takes it to the secret room to place it with the earlier cloth.

The wizard taps on the bottle as a wake-up call to the occupant. Whoever it is must not be responding. The wizard says, "Keep knocking on the side of the bottle while I watch for any sign of movement." He bends over to look inside. "Continue the knocking."

Vyruss wonders, *Should I use the poker to give a sharper sound? No, that may crack the glass.* He continues to use his knuckles.

The wizard holds up his hand for Vyruss to stop and calls into the mouth of the bottle, "Reach up and hold on to my hands." The wizard's arms are into the bottle as far as they can go.

Vyruss is alert to the wizard's need. He runs to the other end of the table, puts his arms around Griswold's waist, and pulls. *I hope he has a firm grip on his guest and the bottle doesn't move.*

It works. All three fall over backwards onto the carpet in one flurry of arms and legs and heads and bodies. All three quickly pick themselves up, scramble to their feet, and simultaneously straighten themselves. Vyruss discovers that the unknown lunch guest is…not a man…but a woman!

MAKING ACQUAINTANCE

The woman who just emerged from the bottle is unsteady on her feet, and the two men hold out arms to assist her. They help her to the nearby chair. Slender in build, she is well beyond teen age, but not yet middle-aged. Her light brown hair is tied back from a very pale face. She has not seen the sun for over a thousand years. Her clothing is what would be worn when riding sidesaddle on horseback.

She eases back into the chair and rubs and blinks her eyes. Her eyes search the room. Movement becomes easier as she stretches and wriggles her body in the chair. Her face is contorted as she swallows and tries to clear her throat. Vyruss offers her a glass of water.

She gives him a grateful look and sips slowly. It is sweet to her taste. She finds it difficult to speak. "Who...who are you? What time is it? What year is it?" Her voice is soft, well-modulated, educated. She does not have to ask where she is. That she knows full well.

The wizard smiles and says in a kindly tone, "Ma'am, just gather yourself a moment or so, and then we will be glad to answer all your questions. You have been asleep a long while, and all this will be new to you. While you absorb your new surroundings and situation, my friend and I will tidy the room a little."

He brings the small side table with the basin and the ewer closer to the woman and indicates the washcloth and towel. "We are planning a simple meal for the three of us in about an hour. Will that be convenient for you?"

The woman is clearly not yet fully sensible to what has suddenly happened to her, but she nods agreement. Picking up the hand mirror, she looks at herself and pulls in a breath. She is hardly pleased with what she sees.

Griswold motions Vyruss to the far end of the green bottle on the table. They will return it to the hideaway room behind the fireplace. After it is replaced on the trestles, the wizard looks around. He sees nothing else that needs to be returned. Reaching up to the mantelpiece, he pulls the lever to close the back of the fireplace. With his foot, he roughly replaces the fire tongs and grate in their previous position.

Going over to the woman, he says, "We shall leave the room for a spell to allow you time to freshen yourself up. We shall join you after a few moments and seek to respond to your questions." He nods to Vyruss and they slip out the door into the corridor. While there, the wizard gives meal orders to the head steward.

The servant is relieved to know at last what is needed and when and hurries away towards the kitchen.

Vyruss has courteously kept himself from staring at the woman, but he is sure from his brief glimpses that he recognizes her. "Sir, is she…?"

The wizard quickly puts up his hand, but nods his head and smiles. "Shhh! The walls have ears. Just allow things to develop as they will. Don't forget, you must remember everything." They stand for a while discussing things of no importance. Glancing at his watch, Griswold moves to the door and knocks gently. "May we come in?"

A muffled, "Yes, come in," can be heard from inside. The new guest has finished a brief toilette. She washed her face and combed and lightly brushed her hair. Now released, it falls to her shoulders. There are traces of red in it. Feeling a bit more steady, she stood and gave her ankle-length dress a shake or two. Now reseated, she is already more at ease and color is returning to her cheeks.

As they rejoin her, she smiles uncertainly. *I'm not sure what to expect from either of them. The older man presided over my bottling and I know full well who he is. I have good reason to be afraid of him. I have no idea at all who the younger man is.*

The wizard rings the bell and the steward bustles in. He stops suddenly as he sees three people present, not two. *Where did the woman come from? I'm quite certain that no one came up from below.* A look of sudden recognition flashes across his face.

The wizard gives him a stern warning look, and his face quickly becomes as blank as before. "Dispose of the used toiletry items and bring tea for three, at once."

The wizard bows his head towards the new arrival. "Ma'am, you will have many questions for us and we shall do our best to answer them for you. I see you have recognized me, but let me introduce you to the Honorable Dr. Vyruss Tyfuss, Ambassador of Gyminge to the Beyond. Dr. Tyfuss is a soldier, a scholar, and a doctor of quite exceptional experience and skills. He is also resourceful and able. However, he is by nature very modest and retiring. I hope that as time passes, you will become friends. He has a characteristic that I am sure will be attractive to you. Dr. Tyfuss tells the truth, and this is why he has been selected to represent Gyminge abroad. Unfortunately these days, you find this gift in few men indeed. It is a troubling thought. So few people can be trusted, but you can believe what he says at all times.

"I say 'these days,' but I forget that you are unaware what these days are. We are now, ma'am, into the twenty-first century so you have been asleep a long while. You will recognize this room. It has changed little from when you lived here, but I can assure you the world in which you now find yourself is vastly different from what you ever knew. You asked the time of day. It approaches two o'clock in the afternoon.

"Before I invite you to ask us questions, allow me to indicate your living arrangements while you are among us. You will be an honored guest. I am not anticipating you will return to your former place of abode. I have taken the liberty of arranging one of the adjacent guest suites for you together with a personal servant to assist you. Her name is Annie, and although she is deaf and dumb, she is very intelligent and can be completely trusted. Although I must ask you to regard the rest of the castle as off-limits, consider yourself free to use the suite and this room and the porch freely while you are here with us."

The wizard talks quietly, seeking to set his guest somewhat at ease. "All of your previous clothing that was stored away has been placed in your room. Annie sorted some of it into the wardrobe and awaits your instructions on the other items. Much of it will probably no longer be fashionable. Although Gyminge has not been carried along at the same pace of change as the Beyond, changes in fashion and style have certainly occurred here as well. Annie can readily see to any clothing that needs repair or alteration or washing, starching, and ironing. If you have any further needs, kindly communicate them to me and I will see what can be done."

Vyruss studies the woman carefully. It interests him that her hair has not grown while she slept. A quick glance confirms that neither have her fingernails. Her face is oval with light brown eyes widely spaced. Her ears are small and close to her head. When she smiles, traces of dimples appear. Her mouth has a tendency to turn up rather than down. She appears to be of average height, about the same height as Vyruss himself. She wears what any countrywoman might have worn in her day—an undistinguished, tight-necked, rose-colored, laced bodice with a grey, full-length skirt. It is not royal attire, but he thinks, *I believe she was the queen during my childhood.* He can only hazard a guess at her age. If she is indeed the queen, then she had a daughter who would have been in her mid- or late teens. That is likely to make her close to forty if not older.

He notices that, unlike the women servants who bustle around the castle, she is quietly serene and composed even in the way she sits. It gives her a sense of poise and inner peace whatever the outward circumstances might be.

As yet, the wizard has not given his guest any opportunity to ask questions. "I think, ma'am, that in welcoming you and introducing ourselves, I have answered your initial questions, but undoubtedly, you will have more."

He is interrupted by the steward bringing the tea. Griswold apologizes, "Well, my dear lady, perhaps your questions will have to wait while we enjoy tea. Would you care to pour?"

THE LADY ASKS QUESTIONS

It is apparent at once that the new guest is accustomed to the courtesies of afternoon tea. While the lady pours the tea, little is said other than pleasantries. She serves first the wizard, then Vyruss, and finally herself.

Vyruss is hungry; it has been a long time since he had a good meal. *I wish there were sandwiches as well as the Jaffa cakes and Digestive Biscuits on the tray.* He comforts himself with the thought, *I shouldn't spoil my appetite since I know a meal is on the way.* He limits himself to three of each.

It is to Vyruss that she addresses her first question. The wizard's reputation for truthfulness has never existed. If she is to find out anything, it is more likely to come from the stranger even though the wizard's commendation is probably false and a trick. "Do you know what has happened to my husband and daughter, Dr. Tyfuss?"

Vyruss thinks hard, trying to recollect what he does know. "Ma'am, am I right to understand you refer to King Rufus and the princess, Alicia? I heard something new today about the king from my friend here, but he can share that with you. I heard that there was a fierce battle at Fowler's Bridge when we were invaded by the troops from Wozzle. It was there that the king was badly wounded in the fighting. Before he could be captured, he was carried off to the Beyond on the back of an eagle. Years later, I heard that the king never recovered from his wounds and that he died somewhere in the Beyond. Until this afternoon, I believed that to be true. That was all I knew about the king.

"As for Princess Alicia, my understanding is that she fell from the walls of the castle into the lake and was drowned. Pieces of her clothing were found, but I never heard that her body was recovered. As far as I know, she is dead as well. I am so sorry to have to tell you this."

The lady's heart sinks within her at this news. *I've been hoping so desperately to see them both again one day.*

But Vyruss continues, "For that matter, ma'am, I also heard that you were dead. However, I am glad to see that is incorrect. Perhaps my other information is also incorrect."

She doesn't express her thoughts, but thinks, *I am impressed with the way my question has been answered. It was as though the young man was searching his mind for anything that would help me towards the truth about my family. I like his open face.* She turns to look at the wizard, waiting for him to expand on what Vyruss just said. *Perhaps he will have better news.*

Griswold clears his throat. "Queen Sheba, until recently, I also believed that both your husband and daughter were dead. I have no more news of your daughter than Dr. Tyfuss, so I cannot give you any comfort there. Some torn and blood-stained clothing was indeed recovered from the lake and was identified as being from the royal wardrobe of the princess. It may even be in the Royal Museum, and if so, I will have it brought to you. Perhaps you can identify whether or not it is actually your daughter's clothing, but it does seem that she is dead. I regret having to confirm this sad news.

"However, news of your husband is a little more hopeful. I myself saw your husband leaving on the back of an eagle while the battle for this castle was still going on. They were heading south. That was many centuries ago. Nothing had been heard of him since. Had he lived, he surely would have been active in attempts to regain what was once his. I had indeed been expecting that, and when it never happened, I assumed he must have died from his wounds.

"A small band of rebels escaped at that same time. I know where they live in the Beyond, and they are all well-known to me. However, I am quite certain that the king, even in disguise, has never been among them. That was the situation until Saturday, just two days ago when I was in the rebel residence in the Beyond on State business, I encountered, although not face-to-face, two individuals. Both were our size, not Beyonder-size. One was a schoolboy wearing spectacles that I have come across previously. He is a Beyonder, although I believe the other was not.

"The other, I only saw his back, was a man with red hair and a limp. His name was Cydlo. As far as I recollect, that is the only time I have ever seen him. However, upon reflection, I think that it is likely he is King Rufus, reemerged from I do not know where.

"Ma'am, I noticed you started with surprise when I mentioned the name Cydlo. May I ask whether that name means anything to you?"

The queen pauses to think about her answer. *Is the wizard fishing for confirmation that this man is my husband? Is this why he brought me out of the bottle? Will my answer set an awful train of events in motion? But if I expect truth from the doctor, even if not from the wizard, I must not fail to respond with it.* In actual fact, she can only answer truthfully. She could not do otherwise; the Twith do not lie.

She answers, "Yes, it does mean something to me. Cydlo Castle is the castle where I grew up in Wozzle before my family moved to Gyminge. I also went there with my husband several times after we were married, but I don't know whether that would have anything to do with the name of the man you saw in the Beyond. I have heard of more than one man called Cydlo."

The wizard nods. "Yes, I know of Cydlo Castle in Wozzle. And you are right, although the name is unusual, it is not all that uncommon."

The queen is not completely at ease. *The wizard is just far too smooth and clever. By comparison, I could even find myself liking the young man with him. I'm so grateful that I'm not alone with the wizard. The young man will surely prevent any attempt the wizard might make to harm me.*

She continues her questions. "Dr. Tyfuss, where do you fit into this situation and why have I been brought out of my bottle at this particular time?"

"Ma'am, I am appointed to take a message to King Rufus in the Beyond, assuming that this Cydlo that my friend encountered is indeed the king. If he is not, I shall not deliver my message. I shall have to return with my errand incomplete. It is planned that I will leave tomorrow morning for the southern border. Then I will go on into the Beyond. I am to return by noon on Wednesday with his answer. I do not yet know what the message is that I am to take, but I am assured I shall know in good time.

"My friend here can better answer your second question. I myself only arrived here at noon today from the south. However, I do believe that he means you no harm. He has already assured me that if you wish to send your husband a letter by my hand, the writing materials are over there on that table. You may write what you wish and seal the envelope securely with the sealing wax. No one will make any attempt to read what you have written.

"Before I conduct any of my official business with the king, if he is indeed the king, I shall give him your letter and wait until he has read it. I give you my word, ma'am, that even if my friend here asked me to hand over your letter to him, I would not do so. If you choose to place such a letter in my hands, it will be delivered to the person to whom you address it in exactly that same condition as when you hand it to me. If it is not possible to deliver it, the letter will be returned to you unopened."

The wizard nods agreement with all that Vyruss has said. He waits to see if the queen wishes to question Vyruss further about his answers.

Instead, she asks, "When is the latest that such a letter must be ready? I will indeed wish to write to my husband, but there will be much to say."

The wizard smiles and answers for the doctor. "Dr. Tyfuss will be leaving here in the company of the mail messenger immediately after breakfast at eight o'clock in the morning. You may place it into his hands as he leaves, and that will be soon enough."

There is a knock on the door. The wizard answers. The head steward and several lesser stewards bustle in behind him. All carry trays heavily laden with bowls whose contents are steaming happily.

Vyruss smiles in anticipation. *At last! Lunch is about to be served. I'm hungry enough to eat a horse. Well, a pony anyway.*

BREAKFAST FOR THREE

King Haymun has not enjoyed the weekend. He had a troubled night in his four-poster bed haunted by disturbing dreams of invading Chinese on the rampage jumping from the walls of the castle into the lake with him as their prisoner. He doesn't sleep as well now that he has given up twirling his teething ring on his big toe, even though his right toe is available and his left toe has healed.

However, it is not only lack of sleep that disturbs him. He grumbles unhappily. "The wizard is ignoring me. I am, after all, second in command in the kingdom. Although that interfering raven seems to think that he is, there's certainly nothing official about that. He constantly gets between me and the wizard. Now, matters of State are going on in the wizard's apartment, and I have been excluded. After hundreds of years of loyal service! That hurts. To add insult to injury, my former physician—who is most certainly a subordinate to myself—has been involved in these matters of State in preference to me.

"Am I, the king of the goblins, slipping? Has the wizard decided upon a change of monarch? Is Dr. Tyfuss being groomed as my successor? All kinds of recent minor incidents loom large with frightening implications. Although I haven't yet caught a glimpse of her, there is quite clearly a woman in the apartments. There's no other reason for Annie to be on duty there. What exactly is going on? As the monarch, I have a right to know!"

He had his breakfast early and is sitting out of sight in the corner of his bedroom with the window onto the porch wide open. He holds an open book, but he is not reading. Instead, he attempts to overhear the conversation between the wizard and Dr. Tyfuss. Although he listens intently, he only hears a few words now and again. The busy bridge building across the lake under Sergeant Pimples is far noisier than it needs to be.

Sitting on the porch facing each other are the wizard and his new ambassador. Speaking softly, the wizard reads aloud the letter he has written to King Rufus. "I seek your opinion, Mr. Ambassador." By now, the wizard is regularly addressing Vyruss as Mr. Ambassador. "Does it give the right measure of firmness and at the same time suggest a readiness to negotiate?"

Vyruss affirms that it does, "Yes, sir. You have made it perfectly clear."

Griswold continues, "On minor matters, you, as my official ambassador, are authorized to proceed without further approval from me. The major issue is that the rebel Twith and their king must affirm they are not cheating me. There is to be no trickery this time. The Book of Lore must be complete with no omissions or alterations. They must give their word that the book contains nothing but the Lore and nothing less than the Lore. Only then can the rest of the deal go ahead.

"If the king agrees to the terms suggested in my letter, and it is hard to see why he wouldn't do so, then no time should be wasted. The handover must be at the border somewhere. Avoid the bog and choose another location with easy access from dry land. Before leaving the Brook, go yourself and confirm the exact location. The rebels must then return you to the waterfall and one of their birds should await your return within an hour or so."

The wizard explains to Vyruss the other arrangements. "Once Rasputin delivers you to the farmhouse and gives my message to Mrs. Squidge, he will come back and report to me that his part of the task is complete. He will then return to the southern border and wait for you. I remind you, you need to be there by noon on Wednesday. There will be no need for you to bring news of the negotiations back to the castle. I will no longer be here. You will let Rasputin know if the terms are agreed, and he will bring the message to me. Once Rasputin is on his way, you must return promptly to the Brook. The less time the rebels have to change their minds, the better. Is all of this clear? It is hard to see how anything can go wrong.

"To avoid loss of time, I will presume that the negotiations on the Brook will be successful. The queen and I will both be traveling to the immigration control center tomorrow morning. We will leave the castle right after breakfast. You can pass the word to the major to expect us. The exchange can take place as soon as dinnertime tomorrow if there are no snags.

"For the exchange itself, you will satisfy yourself that the Book of Lore is indeed the document we are interested in. It is to be placed in a protective waterproof bag. You and the king together will bring it as close to the curtain as you can get and place it on the ground. Then, you will both withdraw forty paces. I will be present on the Gyminge side at least forty paces distant from the curtain. No one else watching either from Gyminge or from the Brook shall be nearer than one hundred paces. I will have my usual appearance and not be disguised as someone or something else. The queen will be with me. She will move forward and present herself alone at the same spot where the Book of Lore is on the other side of the curtain. When she has done so, and has been recognized by the king, it will be time for the next move.

"You will come forward alone, leaving the king where he is. You will pick up the Book of Lore and stand facing the queen with only the curtain between you. Once I am satisfied that the rebel Twith are not playing any tricks, I will briefly open a pair of slits in the curtain. The queen and the Book of Lore will be exchanged simultaneously. You will step through with the Book of Lore at the same time the queen passes through to the other side. As soon as this happens, the curtain will be sealed again. The agreed transaction will be complete. Are there any questions?"

Vyruss is no fool. *I know that the wizard is positioning me as a hostage to be taken by the rebel Twith if there shall be any attempt at trickery. However, I think I know that the wizard is not planning any tricks of his own, just scheming to get hold of the Book of Lore any way he can. The wizard, who trusts nobody, is trusting me to make sure that the Book of Lore he receives is the genuine and complete Lore. Both sides are trusting me to tell the truth. Well, I'll satisfy them both.* He replies, "No, I don't have any questions."

Inside the large sitting room, the queen sits in the writing alcove putting the finishing touches to her long letter. She frequently wipes tears away from her eyes. She has not slept well either. Her mind has been full of disturbing thoughts, including memories of her lost daughter. Occasionally, she glances at the clock and writes more rapidly. Soon she has completed her letter. In her bedroom, she cut a lock of her hair and now she places it carefully between two pages of her letter. This time, the squat little candle is lighted and available to warm the sealing wax. She uses it to secure the flap on the envelope, and presses her initials into the wax using the handle of the pen. Turning it over, she addresses it simply to: *King Rufus, by hand.* She will pass it over to the ambassador only at the last moment.

At the other end of the room, the servants are quietly flitting about, making preparations for breakfast for three.

The wizard comes in from the porch and nods to the steward that breakfast can be brought and served. He finds the queen sitting at the fireplace waiting, She is wearing a different dress from the one she wore yesterday. Her feet are together and her hands folded. The wizard pauses at the writing table, makes no changes to his own letter, and signs it. Placing it within an envelope, he addresses this also to: *King Rufus, by hand.* In addition, he adds: *Private, personal, and confidential.* He seals it with the sealing wax and impresses the castle seal upon it.

Griswold joins the other two at the table and passes the letter quietly to Vyruss without comment. He greets the queen. "I trust you slept well, my dear." Before breaking the first of his two boiled eggs, he turns to the steward. "Advise the guard that the ambassador will be on time at the guardhouse. The escort should be ready to mount and move off as soon as they see him leave by boat from the castle gate."

He grins smugly at Vyruss. "Congratulations, Mr. Ambassador. You have chosen a beautiful day for your journey."

MUSIC ON THE BROOK

While the wizard deals with matters of State back in Gyminge, far different activities are in progress on the Brook and at the farmhouse. Two Twith weddings are being planned for Friday. The two brides, Elisheba and Cymbeline, are radiant while the two brothers they are to marry hardly touch the ground as they walk.

On the Brook itself, most of the matters are highly choral. The toads consider that the musical aspects of this double ceremony are in their domain rather than that of the birds who tend to think themselves as the only choristers on the Brook. The toads were informed of one wedding over a week ago and are getting highly organized. Rehearsals by two different choirs are becoming increasingly competitive. There is even persuasion going on secretly for some of the toad soloists to switch choirs. Buffo leads one choir and his nephew, Bingo, leads the other. Both are keen to have the best sopranos and tenors available. Their choirs try practicing in half a dozen different areas around the bog wherever the acoustics seem to be the best.

The processional from the log entrance at Twith Mansion will proceed to the cowshed where the weddings will take place. The brides and their attendants will walk between long lines of toads. To allow for the maximum number of toads, the processional carpet will be laid in the shape of an *S*, going around the well on the way. The cover of the well is reserved for the best of the toad soloists. It is not yet clear who will make this selection. They will have a good view of the procession the whole way.

Buffo and the toad lyricists want details of which bridal party will lead the way so they can get the lyrics in the right order. When asked, Gumpa just shrugs his shoulders. "I don't know. I'm waiting for gran'ma to sort out the details so I can ask her. Just now, she is far too busy with other things, but I'm working on it."

Meanwhile, through the night, the squelching and burping of the music practice continues. Toads somehow sing better at night. Buffo ventures, "Could the weddings be after dark, gran'ma?"

Gran'ma is quick to veto that suggestion. "Absolutely not! We don't want the brides or their attendants tripping over anything."

He has another idea and corners Stormy. Pleading with her, he says, "We really need choir robes to look presentable for a wedding. Will you get the children busy making them for us?"

Stormy, knowing what gran'ma would say, does not even consult her. "No! We can't make you robes. There is just not enough time to make choir robes for all the toads planning to take part. Even if we had enough cloth and seamstresses were unlimited, we couldn't do it. The weddings are only three days away. No, Buffo. I'm sorry, but it's just not possible."

It is finally settled that although Taymar and Elisheba will marry first, Ambro will go first in the processional with his best man. Ambro has asked Barney to be his best man, but so far Taymar has not told anyone who his best man will be. Gumpa, however, is guessing it will be Jock. There is no longer any discussion as to who will escort Elisheba. It will be Cydlo. Stumpy will escort Cymbeline and he has already fashioned himself a new wooden leg of walnut for the occasion. It is highly polished. He doesn't want to let his niece down.

Buffo wants to do something special for Cymbeline who is a favorite of his. He wonders, *Can I create a wedding oratorio using the robins and blackbirds to strengthen my own rather small number of toad sopranos?* In the end, however, he decides on using a master composition for male voices called *The Bachelor's Lament.* The music takes full advantage of the hundreds of available bass singers. He decides to enlist the children's help to rewrite the words. They change the lyrics from a bachelor lamenting that he never married to an ex-bachelor rejoicing harmoniously from the shores of bachelorhood into the depths of the sea of matrimony. As their hero sails off into the sunset with his new bride, the wind strengthens and the waves increase. Thrilling stuff! No room for sopranos and hardly any tenors, just great rolling waves of bass voices singing deep and low as clouds on the distant horizon gather and the hero is lost to sight forever.

Outside the big plate glass window of the sun porch in the cowshed where the wedding ceremonies will occur, two of the boys work at fixing a wide shelf just above the windowsill. It will allow the rabbits and badgers to have a good view of the wedding. They will look directly across the room at the bride and groom. The shelf is made up of two cupboard doors end to end, and it should take about three rows of rabbits on one section and perhaps two rows of badgers on the other. The other animals will gather in the reception area in Uncle Andy's garden where the newlyweds will meet their guests after the ceremony.

Above these shelves, and slightly behind them, are the rows of stretched wires for the birds. The birds have organized three choirs of their own to warble at the reception. There will be general singing of all the songbirds conducted by the cuckoo. The birds hope that by giving the cuckoo a baton to wave around, he will not join in the singing. He will have a special conducting platform suspended from the eaves. The robins, who rather fancy themselves, have their own quintet. Sparky, the sparrow, has hidden talents in creating choruses and is frantically composing something for the thrushes and the blackbirds to sing together. This is in addition to Buffo's oratorio for the combined bird and toad choirs.

To avoid the magpies spoiling the main choir, they have been asked to develop a magpie skit to be presented at the reception when things have settled down a bit. They are pleased that their acting skills are acknowledged and do not recognize it is because anything is preferable to their singing.

Down at the cottage, Mrs. Squidge hears the heavy beat of the ragtime rhythm the toads practice night after night. She is unaware of the reason for the noise, but the burping of the toads in their hundreds disturbs her rest. She wants to scream, "Don't toads ever sleep?" The bog is developing a movement of its own. The simultaneous downbeat of toad feet squeezes the bog matter and creates a sucking sound. As the rhythm slowly builds, the sounds assist each other like muffled echoes. This might well be enough disturbance to turn the bog not just into peat, but hard coal!

Except for the toads, Squidgy is enjoying the peace and calm of her empty cottage. She reviews the events of the past few days. "I wasn't too pleased to see my sister show up unexpectedly last week. Frijji looked very alluring and captured the wizard's attention more than I liked. Then Griswold invited the circus to come to the Brook. MY! What a lot of confusion that caused. I was surprised that my yeast buns changed Moley, the mole king, into a Zebrotter. But the wizard turned him into the star of the circus as the Masked Menace from Madagascar, champion weightlifter. And he transformed Frijji into a schoolgirl so she could join the circus as well. I was glad when dear Griswold sent the goblin king back to Gyminge with all his troops. And then Saturday morning, he left and never returned. I would have thought he would at least have stopped in to say good-bye." Squidgy gives a little sigh of disappointment.

"Ah, well! Now that the circus has left, everything has settled down like a lullaby after a nightmare. Frijji and Moley decided to stay with the circus and they are both on their way to Dover." The Cornish woman chuckles delightedly. "I cleverly sent Growler, Frijji's Great Dane, chasing after her. Good riddance to him! That completed the emptying out of visitors. Thankfully, none of them have returned.

"I haven't seen Rasputin around, and Jacko—that sneaky ferret—is living where the goblin troops lived before they were ordered back to Gyminge. Ignoring the six titchy pterodactyls on the ridge of my roof, there are just the three of us at home now—myself, the SnuggleWump, and my sweet little kitty cat. Cajjer is such a comfort to me. It's like the good old days when we first arrived on the Brook."

Contrary to Squidgy's opinion of him, Cajjer is not exactly sweet. He is bad-tempered, scratches and bites, and is just plain mean.

Mrs. Squidge is a bit proud of her accomplishment in creating the SnuggleWump that lies across the path to her cottage. She reflects, "He was my very first transformation. In his early, very ordinary days, he was a plain lizard. If it hadn't been for my timely intervention, he would have been an unknown lizard all his life. When he died, he wouldn't have been missed by anyone, except perhaps a few baby lizards.

"Because of me, he became a twin-headed dragon of huge size with long, sinuous necks and only one eye in each head. I've seen them flash bright red when he is angry. But mostly they stay a cool green." She gives a little sigh. "The poor creature. He started off with two pairs of ears, but owing to accidents beyond my control, he is down to one ear on each head. I named him SnuggleWump because he was so frightening when I first saw him. Mum used to yell at us that the SnuggleWump would come eat us up if we didn't behave and I was sure that's what the creature was. However, he has been a good watch-guard for me.

"I must admit that his transformation was actually by accident rather than by design. However, I created an ingenious product based on the simple yeast buns of my childhood. My recipe could be used to populate the zoos of the world with extraordinary creatures never before conceived. Even the most brilliant inventors could not design them in their wildest dreams."

Squidgy is disappointed with the wizard. "I had been hoping for a letter in the mail from my friend across the border. I was sure dear Griswold would explain what happened to him. After all, we are close allies. However, my trips to the post office have yielded nothing except advertisements for double-glazed windows. Don't they know this is a listed building? I can't make any changes like that.

"Tonight, when no one is around, I will take a turn around the Brook on my broomstick. Cajjer can come along for the ride. I'll see if I can nose out what is going on. Then I'll drop a note to the wizard, letting him know what the situation is. When I did that thirty years ago, he didn't waste any time coming to see me." She has already forgotten that she is content with no visitors in the house.

RASPUTIN ON THE BROOK

Over in Gyminge, the Ambassador of Gyminge to the Beyond arrives at the southern border. He informs Major Bubblewick, "Some *very* important visitors are due to arrive in twenty-four hours."

The major's face turns an ashy grey. He looks at his watch and goes into a complete tizzy. *Accommodations for guests are by no means even half ready. Night is coming all too soon. My men are not going to get any rest this night, and neither am I!*

Rasputin arrives at the border but has no further news from the castle.

Vyruss has more instructions for the major. "An hour and a half before dawn, I want you to send twelve goblins with lamps into the tunnel. They are to space themselves evenly along the length of the tunnel, set their lamps on the floor, and then stand beside them with their backs against the wall. They will remain on duty until I return sometime tomorrow before noon. Come, Rasputin. We better get some rest until then."

Major Bubblewick sighs. *I wish I could rest until then.* He excuses himself. "I need to get my men busy completing the guest accommodations."

Vyruss also sighs. *I doubt I'm going to get much rest with construction work going on all night.*

Rasputin has a built-in clock that usually wakes him a half hour before dawn. Before he went to sleep, he alerted himself to awake earlier this morning. He wants to make sure the twelve goblins are on their way with lights for the tunnel. He remembers his first journey through the tunnel to the waterfall. *The goblin that was selected to guide me should never have been allowed within arm's length of a lighted flame. In his haste to get back out of the tunnel, he set me alight, burning my wing feathers. Only a dive into the waterfall pool saved me from becoming a pile of ashes. To make matters worse, it adversely affects my flying ability.*

He mutters to himself unhappily, "If this had been during the Reformation, that particular goblin would have been burned at the stake three times over and then served a life sentence in jail to teach him a lesson. It is not going to happen this time. I'm not going into that tunnel until the goblins have taken their lights and positioned themselves well in advance. After they have set their lamps on the floor and are standing beside them, then I intend to fly through, not walk. The sooner I'm through, the better. Vyruss can make his own way at his own pace. I'll just wait in the hawthorn tree beyond the waterfall for the new ambassador to make his appearance. I'll give him my promise that I will pick him up as soon as he steps through the curtain."

Rasputin has his plan for what happens after that clear in his mind. *Success depends on precise timing. Once I have Vyruss in my claws, I will not head straight to the farmhouse. The eagle's nest in the oak tree is straight on the route. No, I'll stay low, fly south over the croc' pond, and down the path towards Squidgy's cottage. The enemy owl keeps watch from the ash tree there, but I won't go that close. I'll turn east before he can spot me and fly low over the barley field towards the farmhouse. I can drop to a landing somewhere near the sycamore tree. Once I've delivered the ambassador, it will be low and fast back over the barley field to Squidgy's cottage. I'll deliver the wizard's letter, and then head back to the waterfall before the light of day. I'll have a good three quarters of an hour, which should be more than enough time.*

Rasputin, like the wizard, is unaware that Vyruss has previously visited the bog. Although the bird saw Vyruss there recently, he did not recognize him. When the raven spotted the ex-doctor in danger of drowning in the bog, the man was wearing a face mask and a sheet adapted as a surgical gown. Those were not the best togs in which to be recognized and helped by a friend flying overhead, especially when the raven was busy rescuing somebody else who was more important—the goblin king.

Before leaving this morning, Rasputin goes to the mess tent for a final rendezvous with the ambassador. Vyruss and Major Bubblewick are just finishing a substantial breakfast of fried eggs on bubble and squeak. The new Commander of the Southern Zone looks as though he has been dragged through a hedge backwards. He has been almost twenty-four hours without sleep and is fretful. *It has not been a particularly fruitful night getting work done. I wish the wizard would appoint me to be an ambassador too. I also wish Colonel Tyfuss would hurry up and be on his way so that I can catch a few moments' sleep.*

Vyruss wipes his lips on his napkin, pats his tummy, checks the time, finishes off his apple juice, and rises. He checks his letters. All three of them are safe within his inside pocket. The pocket has a top button to keep them secure. Even though ambassadors and dispatch cases go together like bread and jam or boys and mud, a dispatch case of any kind would be one piece of luggage too many. He will be traveling awkwardly by bird, and he will need both hands free to raise the flag. He picks up his flag from the corner of the tent as he exits.

The ex-doctor has been thinking ahead. During his studies of woodlouse behavior, he has observed that thinking ahead is one of their characteristic traits. He has taken the practice to heart. Vyruss is thinking of what will happen to his flag as it passes through the waterfall. *I should have brought a waterproof cover. I don't want a sopping wet flag drooping around its pole when I make my dramatic reappearance at Twith Mansion. The flag needs to be bone dry, flying straight and proud in the light breeze, catching the gold of the rising sun, a concerto in black and white.*

When I leave, I'll carry the flag like a lance, at a slight angle upwards so that the flag does not touch the ground. But if I reverse the flag, I can tuck it under my coat as I walk through the waterfall.

He thinks about how he might achieve that. *I could do that while I'm in the tunnel by walking to the front of the flag and tucking the flag under my coat. That means the pole of the flag will be sticking out behind me. That could present problems as I try to negotiate my way down the bank and turn to head towards the opening in the curtain at the waterfall. It could even prod me into the waterfall pool if I am off balance. On the other hand, if I wait to sort out the flag after I arrive at the waterfall, the flag will be ahead of me. Will I be able to avoid having the flag swing through the waterfall in the process? I hope it is not raining on the Brook.*

It is time to be moving. "Major, I must be on my way. I was instructed by the wizard to leave not less than an hour before dawn. Although there are still a few moments until then, there may be snags along the way. I want to remind you that it is possible the visitors from the castle may arrive at an earlier time than I did yesterday. After all, I journeyed quite slowly."

This is not good news for the major. He feels sick to his stomach. "Well, good-bye then. I'll not accompany you to the toad tunnel. I need to ensure the men are working full speed ahead."

He throws a despairing look towards his own tent and groans as if in great pain. Reluctantly, he makes his way back to where his exhausted troops are whitewashing everything in sight. Since it is dark, there are items they are missing that they will have to return to when dawn comes. This is normal army procedure.

At the cave-tunnel, the long straight tunnel is dim but adequately lit. The guards beside their lamps throw still shadows. None of them move. They saw the arrivals at the entrance and await their progress past them.

Rasputin calls out, "I'll see you on the Brook," and is off like a flash before Vyruss can even say, "Hey!" It is a tunnel big enough for full-size mother toads, and although Rasputin doesn't try it, he could possibly loop the loop as he flies. There is plenty of room for the bird to maneuver, and he congratulates himself. "Well done, my lad. At last, you've solved the problem of a bird's safe transit through this tunnel."

The lamp at the very end throws back flashes of reflected light in all colors from the splashing stream that leads to the waterfall. This particular lamp is cared for by the goblin who almost drowned in the waterfall pool on a previous occasion and nearly strangled the sergeant major in the process. He is a non-swimmer and is staying well back from the end where the path trails down the bank. He is not happy. "I can't figure out how it happened that I'm at this end of the tunnel instead of the other end. It must be because I'm not as smart as the others." He concludes correctly on that one. He sighs. "At least, I'm smarter than my twin brother. He couldn't even enroll in the army because he couldn't sign his own name." He does a bit of rethinking. "I'm not that sure which of us is smartest. Maybe literacy isn't all that hot after all. Look where it's gotten me."

Rasputin lands, and as he walks carefully past the last lamp, he calls out a farewell. Finding the path down the bank, he launches out towards the bog. As he passes through the curtain, he experiences the sudden shock of enlargement. He coughs for breath. *I must remember not to caw. I don't want to attract any attention.*

As he searches for a landing branch, he hears a strange burping beat. "What is that awful noise? It seems to be coming from the pulsing of the surface beneath me. It is as though the bog has a stomachache."

VYRUSS TAKES FLIGHT

Vyruss takes it slow and easy through the tunnel, not hurrying. He doesn't want to bang his head when the roof dips. The lights are a great help. He carefully steers the flag he carries ahead of him around each of the lamp guards.

He reassures himself. "I'm heading off towards secret friends, so I'm not worried about the assignment that lies ahead. In fact, I am rather looking forward to it. It will be a good challenge for me."

Growing inside of him is a sense of high destiny. "This is when the world finds out why Vyruss Tyfuss was born. I can see in my mind's eye the initials VT that have been carved in the bark of oak trees all across the Brook by approving followers. I can even hear the distant clamor of the mobs in the Square, 'Vote for VT, Vote for VT.' This is my moment in time.

"I'm responsible for negotiations between two bitterly opposed enemies—the wizard and the Twith. They are like armies determined to destroy each other. Ah! But between the massed battle lines arrayed for conflict, there is a slight figure holding a white flag. Well, almost white. The mediator! The hope of the people, none other than Vyruss Tyfuss himself. My long studies of the habits of woodlouses have not been in vain. Men are little different than woodlouses when you really get down to it."

He muses sadly, "If only I had been at Waterloo! Think of the wives who would not have been widowed and the children who would not have been orphaned. The horses would still have their riders and the pensions not gone unclaimed." He sighs. "What this world needs is more men of peace, like myself, and less violence."

Carried away by his thoughts, he moves on to the battle of Hastings. *If I had been the referee, I would have insisted that the two forces remain one and a half arrow shots from each other. As for the Battle of the Somme, they failed to call the quiet man they needed. The hundreds of thousands of casualties in that battle occurred because I was not there to pour oil on troubled waters with a few words of cool, calming wisdom.*

He ducks instinctively as his tall, black hat brushes the dipping roof. Both his hat and his black overcoat have been furnished by the wizard from his own wardrobe. "Stay alert, Vyruss," he warns himself. "There must be no accidents. Oh! I can hear the splashing of the water ahead. I'm getting close to the end of the tunnel at last."

The last goblin, forgetting his intent to remain stock-still, snaps to attention and flings a salute. The ambassador sees it coming and ducks fast, temporarily losing his hat. He picks it up and pulls it back on tight.

Emerging from the tunnel, Vyruss walks over to the bank leading down to the waterfall. It is not a gentle slope, and he remembers that he skidded partway down on his last trip this way. He is concerned about his flag. "I wonder, should I toss it down the bank instead of trying to carry it? No, I better not. It might roll off into the pool and get so soaked. I'd never get it dry." A bright idea hits him. "I know what I'll do! It'll use the pole as a walking stick. That will aid my descent so I won't slip. It will get the end dirty but I can wash it off in the pool." Slowly and carefully, he makes his way down the bank to the landing on the Gyminge side of the waterfall. It is still dark and difficult to see anything.

Rasputin has been watching the waterfall from his perch in the hawthorn tree. He peers intently. "I'm not sure, but I think I see a thin pole making a wriggling arc beyond the waterfall. It keeps disappearing behind the sheet of water." He blinks and leans forward. Thinking that perhaps the ambassador may be about to emerge, he lunges into the air.

Vyruss steps forward uncertainly as he comes through the curtain onto the landing on the Brook side. Somehow, he managed to maneuver his flagpole underneath his overcoat, although it still got wet and he now clutches a slightly soggy flag to his chest. He is uncomfortable and feeling a bit helpless. He grumbles to himself, "I wish I had extra hands and arms! I need one to hold on to my hat, one to clutch the flag, and one to guard it with my overcoat. I also need another one to steer the flagpole so that it doesn't point itself either into the bog or into Rasputin."

He hardly sets foot on the bog before he is snatched up by Rasputin grabbing a shoulder in each claw. Vyruss involuntarily yells, "OUCH!" He feels the sharp pain of the raven's claws digging into his shoulders. "I'm glad I have this thick overcoat to soften some of the pain of his grasp. Actually, I'm quite glad he has a firm grip on me. I don't want to have him drop me into the bog. I've been there and it wasn't fun."

The bird remembers the wizard's instructions and is determined to fulfill his part of the mission. "My job is to deliver the ambassador to the farmhouse and then deliver a message to Mrs. Squidge. I'm not going to let my master down or the ambassador either. We may go down, but it will be together, not separately.

To secure the wizard's hat against blowing off, Vyruss once more pulls it down tight. He has pulled the brim just above his eyes, and he can now only see downwards. Since it is dark, that is not too important for the moment.

Vyruss wonders, *What on earth is that noise? It's like the rumbling of a deep earthquake, or thick mud squeezing itself painfully through a plughole, or a lava flow from a volcano. Whatever it is, it has a rhythm, a beat to it. Ah! I remember now! That's something I've heard before. It was when I fled from the emergency operating tent in Blindhouse Wood. I had a fleeting glimpse of hundreds of fat toad bellies. They were loudly burping a marching song.*

The Toads are on the road,
What's better than a Toad?
We hop and jump,
We skip and bump,
We Toads are on the road!

"The toads must be up to something. But what? Where are they going now? Why so early in the morning?"

Rasputin is highly pleased with himself. "My timetable is working perfectly. I've snatched the ambassador off the bog as planned. Fortunately, he has the bottom end of the flagpole pointing straight forward in the direction of flight. I was fearful that he might spear me with it, but everything is going well." The raven heads low over the bog towards the croc' pond. Once there, he will veer in direction to fly down the path towards Squidgy's cottage.

SQUIDGY TAKES FLIGHT

Unknown to Rasputin, other activity besides the toads' choir practice is taking place near the bog.

Last evening, Mrs. Squidge decided she would take an unscheduled, very early morning flight to survey what is going on around and about the Brook. She prefers to fly when it is still dark to avoid attracting attention from the neighbors. Sellindge is a village of gossips. Her excuse for the trip is to report her findings in a letter to the wizard. She hopes by doing so, he will respond by coming to visit.

It is nearly dawn before she gets ready. This is not by intent, but because she overslept. Not only that, but one of her shoelaces broke. She tied the ends together and is hurriedly lacing up her leather boots. She mutters to herself, "I need to be on my way. It will soon be light." Pulling on the new cloak her sister brought from Cornwall, she fastens it tightly at the neck. "I don't want to lose this one in some unplanned aerial maneuver the way I did the last one."

The old woman has a form of transport that is now less usual than it used to be. She flies on a twig broom. In the old days, more people used to ride on brooms than on bicycles. Earlier this summer, her old broom got out of control. She was forced to release it, and it headed over towards Paris. Fortunately, she did not suffer permanent injury when she landed, although it is possible the broom itself did.

Her sister brought her a new one from a factory in Cornwall that has received high acclaim from experts in flying brooms. They only use the very best materials. This broom handle is longer, and the twigs are thicker and longer. It has much more rapid acceleration, and she is not yet completely accustomed to its higher power and more sensitive maneuverability.

Squidgy chuckles to herself. "I'm going to fool the watching owl this time. I'll take off from inside the house, swing low, and to the left up the path before the owl has time to blink an eye." She turns all the lights out in the cottage. Inch by slow inch, she eases the door open. She calls out to her licorice swirl cat, "Cajjer, come get on the broomstick with me."

Sometimes, when the sun is well up, the day is fair, and it is warm and clear, Cajjer is very anxious to join her for a trip. Today, he is not so keen. It is always darkest just before dawn, and there won't be any sightseeing. As he passes the open door, he sniffs the air. *I have a feeling there is going to be rain.* His tail straightens itself like a poker. It, too, has a strange apprehension of events to come. Cajjer mounts the broomstick in his usual place—in front of and just touching the bent knees of his mistress. He is nervous. His inner sense that all is not well, and may get worse, grows stronger all the time.

Squidgy has her route already clear in her head. She tells Cajjer, "Instead of heading in a clockwise direction towards the farmhouse as I usually do, I'll confound anyone who might be watching by going in the reverse direction. I'll fly low up the path towards the croc' pond and then across the bog almost to the waterfall. When I get there, I'll turn towards Cope farm and fly low across the barley fields to the field behind the farmhouse where the circus was held. In case that eagle is on the roof of the farmhouse, he won't be able see me coming from that direction. And that should be quite close enough for me to see what is going on."

This is not going to be a speed take-off. It is best likened to a slow take-off on a bicycle with a punctured tire rather than a racing start in a bicycle sprint. She pushes down with the soles of her feet, brings her knees together, and tucks her elbows in tightly to her sides lest they catch the doorjambs. The broom gathers motion. Smooth as silk, Squidgy sails through the door without even a graze. The SnuggleWump does not stir or even flicker his eyes as the broom makes a sharp left turn just beyond the porch. *So far so good*, thinks Mrs. Squidge. Things are, however, less happy than they seem.

Tuwhit has been on guard duty at the cottage all night. He expects to be relieved shortly after dawn. Although the dawn chorus of birdsong has not yet begun, one or two half-hearted birdcalls suggest that early risers are trying to wake the others. Tuwhit is always on his toes. He was alerted earlier by lights and sounds of movement in the cottage. He was not yet uneasy. "There is no cause for concern just yet. The wizard and his raven haven't been anywhere near for days. Mrs. Squidge may simply have had an uneasy night and is up earlier than usual." Nevertheless, he stays alert and watches carefully down below for anything unusual. As soon as Mrs. Squidge takes off on her broomstick, Tuwhit tumbles forward off his branch into a low glide and pursues her up the path.

Tuwhit knows that his eagle friend, Crusty, has also been on guard duty all night. They have had a long association working with the Twith Logue and take on themselves the most burdensome tasks of guarding them. They consider the long night watches to be their responsibility. Occasionally, they call reassurance to each other during the quiet hours.

Tuwhit decides to alert Crusty. "Whooo! Whooo!" He screeches a loud warning call, "Things are moving at the cottage!"

Unknown to Squidgy, things have already begun to go wrong with her spy flight. Neither Squidgy nor Cajjer has any idea that approaching them, at the same height, and as black as the night sky itself, is a mean-minded raven built like a torpedo with a beak designed to damage if not completely destroy anything in its way.

Furthermore, he is not alone. He carries in his hanging claws a man blinded by his black hat. The flag he carries is extended straight out and upside down like the black knight jousting before

Henry II and the fair Lady Rosamund at Westenhanger Castle. The difference is that this black knight doesn't have a horse. The ambassador, oblivious to what lies ahead, hopes that by the time he arrives at the farmhouse, the flag will be dry enough to wave in the wind. He is completely in the dark about anything going on above, below, or ahead of him. It is the straight ahead of him that should concern him the most, but below him, there is activity as well.

On the ground, Jacko has finished hunting for the night and slinks his way over to the croc' pond. The ferret is a nauseous creature. He is sneaky and he smells horrible. Some say that not all ferrets stink, but they are probably trying to sell one. Some people who own ferrets say they smell better than dogs or cats. However, all the creatures on the Brook, and that includes Griselda Squidge, agree that Jacko stinks and that he stinks worse than any of the other creatures on the Common.

Jacko is a long, skinny animal with a long neck and a body about as long as from a man's fingertips to his elbow. He has a light-colored undercoat, but his back is darker brown and tan. His forelegs almost look as though they are in the middle of his body when he stretches forward. His tail is about one third as long as his body. His teeth are sharp, and his tiny pointed ears make him look something like a mouse, except that his face markings are distinctive. Once you've seen a ferret, you will never forget what they look like. If a hole is big enough for a rabbit to go through, there's no problem for a ferret like Jacko to wriggle his way through, too.

It wasn't long ago that Jacko lived at Gibbins Brook Farm himself, so he knows a great deal about the people who live there, including the Twith Logue. His owner often took him out ferreting for rabbits, but one day, he put Jacko down a rabbit hole without a leash. The ferret decided he would rather stay in the burrow than go back out. He made a new life for himself and chose a career as a freelance mercenary and spy. He will hire himself out to whoever rewards him the most. So far, the only one interested is the wizard.

Griswold finds the ferret to be a useful ally. It was Jacko who stole the Shadow book from Gerald's office, and he has helped the wizard on other occasions since. He doesn't go off the Brook, and at present, he lives in Mole Hall. It was built to house the more than seven hundred goblins that the wizard had stationed on the Brook for a while. When they left, Jacko took advantage of the situation. As part of his deal with the wizard to provide information regarding the location of the Book of Lore, he now has free reign in Mole Hall. Because it is near Squidgy's cottage, he is her nearest neighbor.

Mole tunnels are smaller than rabbit tunnels. They are a tight fit for a ferret and Jacko generally avoids them. However, there is a new series of connected mole tunnels that lead from Mole Hall as far as the croc' pond. Jacko has squeezed through them enough times that he can manage the journey fairly easily. From there, a new long tunnel heads off towards Cope farm along the edge of the bog. That one he hasn't tried out yet.

Jacko reaches the croc' pond where he will wait for light to break into the eastern sky. He finds a resting spot in the undergrowth on a gently sloping bank. Crossing his feet, he puts his paws behind his head and waits for the warmth of the early sun to caress him. He thinks about how much better the world would be if he had twice as much of everything that he already has now. He is not completely hidden in the undergrowth on the north bank of the croc' pond, and he is spotted by Crusty on his way to respond to Tuwhit's warning call that there is activity going on at the cottage.

The lone mallard on the Brook is floating in the middle of the croc' pond. He prefers to be as distant from the bank as possible when the smelly ferret is around. The duck is fast asleep with his head tucked under his wing, dreaming of a meal of worms.

Things are about to get very complicated.

Collision!

If Mrs. Squidge and Rasputin had been trying with stopwatches to coordinate their departures to the second to ensure a collision over the croc' pond, they could not have succeeded any better than they did.

It is similar to two aircraft involved in midair refueling. Because that is not usually done by civilian aircraft, but only by military aircraft, the two planes are both painted in camouflage colors. Each crew is well aware of and out to help the other. Flying east, high over the mid-Atlantic in a clear sky, would be a great lumbering air tanker loaded with fuel. It would fly a straight and steady course at precisely two hundred and fifty miles an hour. Visibility is perfect. Trailing from its tail in a long curve is the fuel hose. At its end is a cone that will only open to permit the flow of fuel once the connection is made and secured.

Below would be the second plane, the one to be refueled, also flying east. To add some excitement, the tiny plane drawing up close behind and below the tanker has only five more minutes of fuel left. At the nose of this twin-engine plane is a slender probe and the pilot guides his probe into the cone to make the essential connection. The speed of the plane is exactly two hundred and fifty one miles an hour.

Suddenly, the two planes enter into a thick cloud. The smaller plane loses its sense of direction as its compass goes bonkers. It is now flying west, not east. It is on a near collision course at over five hundred miles an hour! Wowee! Watch out! Take avoiding action! Hold on to your hat!

It is akin to what happens on the Brook. The collision occurs over the croc' pond. It is not yet dawn and pitch dark. Flying in one direction is the raven. Hanging from his claws is Ambassador Tyfuss. Between them, there is a rectangular opening. At the roof is Rasputin's belly, at the sides are the bird's legs, and on the bottom is the top of the ambassador's hat pulled down tight on his head. Also below is a probe sticking out in front, which is the flagpole that Vyruss holds on to like grim death. It is not horizontal, but pointing slightly downwards. The flagpole is a spear looking for a victim.

In the other direction are, first of all, Squidgy and her cat on the twig broom. The end of her twig broom handle is cocked up at an angle slightly ahead of her. It so happens that it is at exactly the same level as the gap between Rasputin's legs and heading straight for it. Neither Squidgy nor the raven is aware that the other is approaching.

Close behind Squidgy, but a little lower, is Tuwhit. He sees better than any other participant because he has been alert and watchful all night. He is also a predator hunter who needs and has sharp night vision to obtain his food supply.

Several events occur rapidly. First, the rounded end of the broom handle slides neatly between Rasputin's legs and skids a searing furrow along the top of the ambassador's hat, forcing it right off his head. The handle, as it proceeds under Rasputin, also catches the underside of his tail and tilts his body downwards to the angle of the broom handle. His clutch on the ambassador is forced open. This ejects the ambassador like a cork from a bottle of champagne.

No longer held firmly in Rasputin's grasp, Vyruss discovers the supposed joys of free flight. "I think it is highly overrated. There are other things I would rather do." The flagpole penetrates the thickly clustered forest of twigs on the end of the broom. It sticks between them and will go no further. This has a fortunate result. As long as he manages to hold on to the flagpole and it doesn't slip and the broom stays airborne, so will Vyruss. Even if Mrs. Squidge separates, and she has no intention of doing so for one moment, the broom and not Mrs. Squidge is his best hope.

Rasputin's rapid movement down along the broom handle drives his beak into Cajjer. The cat yowls with pain. Recognizing he is about to be scalped, Cajjer rapidly removes himself out of the way with a mighty leap into the air. He didn't take time to make sure there would be something soft to land on. This is a major oversight that he will soon regret.

With Cajjer out of the way, Rasputin's broken beak continues on and strikes Squidgy's upper driving hand. Removing it rapidly, she screams as she feels blood dripping down her arm. Her bloodcurdling yell catches up with and reinforces the cat's wild yowl. Everything that might be sleeping on the Brook is suddenly wide-awake, excluding those up at the farm, which is distant enough that the sound does not carry. The toads are already awake and wonder what has gone wrong with the birds' dawn chorus they have been expecting to hear at any moment.

Squidgy, by removing her bleeding hand, has less control over her broom. Rasputin continues his steady descent along the broom handle and impales her other hand as well. Remembering the attack of the magpies and the loss of her broom into the skies over Paris, she desperately holds on to this broom even though that hand is also seriously wounded.

With her free hand, she whacks at her unknown assailant. With great energy, but merely by chance, she catches Rasputin a beauty on the side of his head. This almost knocks him out of the sky as he sails out into the darkness, whirling and twirling. Being knocked silly, he forgets to flap his wings. His despairing "Caw!" alerts Mrs. Squidge that she may have injured an ally. "Oh well. He started it. And no one is going to push the Cornish around. I'll make certain of that!"

Cajjer's sudden departure had already disturbed the balance of the broom. Now, Rasputin's exit is also unsettling. She wasn't as fully in control of this newer piece of kitchen equipment to begin with as she was her old one. The untested broom and its rider take off for the stars in a rapidly accelerating climb. Squidgy grabs on for dear life with both hands. She may be without either Cajjer or Rasputin, but she is not alone.

Beneath her, although she is unaware of it, hangs a surprised little passenger. He is hatless and his head is sore. Vyruss cannot figure out what is happening. He just received a whacking great bump on his head from the broom handle, so perhaps, that is what affects his ability to think clearly. "The wizard assured me that nothing could go wrong, so everything must be going according to plan. However, he omitted mentioning what is now happening. I may be without headgear, but I'm still wearing the wizard's overcoat. I'm protected against the cold even if not against the rain." At present, it is neither raining or cold. In fact, the ambassador begins to perspire. His thinking clears a little because he realizes, "This is hardly the time or place to be undressing. Although I'm glad to be able to see once more, I can't distinguish a thing as dark as it is. I may have lost my hat, but what really matters is that I'm still holding tight on to the flagpole. The mission is still on."

The broom handle moves away from the top of his head and points more directly upwards. At the moment, all three—the broom, Mrs. Squidge, and her tiny passenger—are heading upwards pursued by two birds below and one above.

One of the birds flying below Squidgy's broom is Tuwhit. He has seen enough to draw an incorrect conclusion as to what is happening. "Hanging on with both hands to a pole wedged into the twigs of Squidgy's broom is a Twith! Most probably, it is Jock's best friend, Jordy. He was on night patrol and must have been picked off by Rasputin. There will be time later to sort out who it might be. Right now, he is swinging wildly to and fro and looks to be in imminent danger of falling. One of the twigs has come loose and is about to detach itself. The important thing is to rescue the wriggling victim before he falls into the bog or is carted off to Gyminge." As he speeds off in hot pursuit, he sounds his screeching battle cry, "Whooo! Whooo!"

The mallard, sleeping so peacefully, is jolted awake by the frantic screech of the owl. Leaving behind his dreams of worm pie, he struggles instinctively into half-flight, fearing attack by wolves. On the spur of the moment, he decides to head to Spain on a holiday. But he doesn't even have time to lift off before he is hit by a falling body that he can't see. As the duck and the cat from above hit the water together, there is an almighty splash. The two creatures submerge together. The mallard struggles to dislodge himself from Cajjer's claws. He remembers the cat by its smell and feel from previous encounters. Once separated, the duck is the better equipped of the two to survive.

The other bird below is Rasputin. He is in despair. "I have failed my master. I don't know how it has happened, but I recognized the simultaneous screams of both Mrs. Squidge and her cat. What on earth, or rather in the air, is she doing flying around without lights this time of the night? She emerged from nowhere and somehow wrested the ambassador from my grasp. If I am ever going to be able to return home without facing trial for mutiny, I have to get the ambassador back and deliver him to the farmhouse as instructed."

The bird above is an eagle. When Crusty heard Tuwhit's warning call, he headed over towards the cottage to satisfy his curiosity. Suddenly he hears a startled "Whooo! Whooo!" from near the croc' pond. Banking sharply, he heads as fast as he can in that direction.

Jacko, half snoozing on the bank below, is lifted vertically by Tuwhit's ear-splitting screech. The horizontal ferret rises a full four feet in the air before he returns to the ground. In that very short flight, Jacko rotates about his long axis and manages to land feet first facing the new mole tunnel. Immediately, he becomes thoroughly drenched by the wave of water being splashed out of the croc' pond by the struggles of the mallard and the cat. For some reason, even though he is on dry land, he thinks he is drowning. He has had a fear of drowning since he was a baby. Just now, he believes his only hope to avoid drowning is to find Noah's Ark before all the other ferrets in Kent do so. He knows only two are going to be allowed in and he intends to be one of them. Noah is one of his heroes, a man who believes ferrets and rabbits can live in close association. Jacko is hungry and is not thinking straight. In his muddled thinking, the mole tunnel is the long covered gangplank leading to the topmost deck of the Ark. He wants to get there before the rabbits arrive. With legs moving at racing speed, the frightened ferret is away from the croc' pond and into the mouth of the mole tunnel that he has not previously explored. Less than halfway into it, the racing ferret becomes stuck. He had no way of knowing that this portion of tunnel would not be as large as the part he barreled through in his race to get to the Ark before all the other creatures clamoring to get aboard.

As Jacko lies on his stomach, panting and trying to catch his breath, he tries desperately to work out how he is going to get forward to the outside again. He is thankful for one thing. At least he can breathe. He needs to be thankful for small mercies. Thinking of the Ark again, he finds himself wondering, *Is it raining torrents outside? Will there be a rainbow?* He is all confused. It promised to be a bright, sunny day. Because he knows how far he has come, there is no way he is going to try to back out. That would take a month of Sundays. He begins to wriggle and nudge himself forwards, an inch or so at a time. It is difficult and exhausting, and he needs to rest frequently. His progress is as slow as a snail's pace, and it will take much time before he reaches the end of the tunnel.

THE AMBASSADOR IN DANGER

Squidgy's motives have been good. But she questions her actions. "So often, when my intentions are pure and lily-white, things go wrong. It makes me sorry I ever thought such kind thoughts in the first place. Kind thoughts often lead to big trouble! All I was doing was trying to be helpful and be a good neighbor as it were. I was only making an inconspicuous, quiet, little anti-clockwise circuit around the Brook. It was just so I could let my friend Griswold, who disappeared without a trace, know what is happening here locally.

"Things went awry almost immediately. Within ninety degrees of my circuit, in fact even before I approached the danger zone up by the farmhouse—I was actually going away from it—I was attacked out of the blue, or rather black, by someone I used to consider a friend. Now, thanks to him, I've lost my cat, perhaps forever." She sniffles unhappily, but can't wipe her nose. "I have cuts on both my hands. I banged my chin on my broomstick only a moment before my forehead received the same treatment. And now, my broomstick has turned into a bucking bronco at a rodeo! It must think it is Pegasus heading for Andromeda."

Mrs. Squidge is completely unaware that below her and trailing behind is the Ambassador of Gyminge to the Beyond. He, poor man, is extremely worried. "I wonder how much longer I can hold on to my flagpole? I'm almost at the limit of my strength, hanging like a piece of washing on the line without clothespins to help." Desperation, and a reluctance to check personally whether the ground below is soft or hard, gives him added incentive and determination. "I have to hold on for a few more moments before

I start unaided flight." He spares no time thinking about wood-louses. "I wonder whether by spreading my arms out wide, my overcoat will simulate bat wings?"

Vyruss is facing backwards, and his face is occasionally wrapped around by the flapping black-and-white flag. Even so, in between flaps, he can occasionally make out the dim silhouettes of the raven and the owl below him. They are racing neck and neck, taking no time out to attack each other. Each is determined to reach him first. He also becomes aware of Crusty whose cackling screech indicates he is preparing to swoop.

Mrs. Squidge, facing the other way, can't see the race in progress behind her. Although she can hear the eagle, she doesn't see where he is and is unaware that he has a definite height advantage.

The ambassador begins to wonder, *Are matters getting out of control?* He is soon to find out. Neither he nor Mrs. Squidge is aware of seven other flying participants about to enter into the confusion that is in progress. Six titchy pterodactyls were alarmed by the screams of their mistress. They all launched into hasty take-offs from the roof of her cottage. "She needs our help! Coming, mistress!" They are in close inline formation, heading lickety-split for the action. They are likely, as they gain height, to cross paths with a mallard who got free from Cajjer's clutches and ascends vertically as rapidly as he can into the confusion above. He incorrectly believes it is empty sky.

The mallard thinks, *The day starts going wrong earlier and earlier the older I get. It must be a sign of old age. It's getting to be that it's safer in the air than on the water.* He just isn't fully awake yet. *Perhaps it is time to consider immigrating to France. Their worms may not be up to much, and they speak a foreign language, but other ducks speak highly of their snails.* The mallard is a peacemaker at heart and concerned only to make his presence heard by honking like a London bus as he works through the traffic.

However, there are three beaks that are ready for conflict. Rasputin's spear-like broken beak will be no match for two hooked beaks designed to tear and pull flesh apart. Also poised for action are six non-beaks, but those six have rows of teeth designed, in the larger edition, to saw through bones as thick as oak trees just for an afternoon snack. All could swallow the ambassador in one gulp. It is just as well the ambassador cannot see what is coming at him.

All the flying creatures involved are making as much noise as they can. Because of their mixed parentage, the teros, even though they were hens, sound like six cockerels crowing their heads off while perched on a steam train entering a tunnel as the driver blows his whistle.

The Brook erupts into the new day with a few moment's silence from the toads. The sounds of birdsong as dawn breaks denotes a thin sliver of light is just below the horizon edging itself upwards in the eastern sky. The bird choir this particular morning is somewhat unsettled and their tunes and harmonies are not as crystal clear as usual.

Over at the cottage, the SnuggleWump, awakened out of his sleep and with no idea what may be happening, begins roaring continuously. Both his heads, red-eyed, are weaving around ready to fend off any attackers. He is on all fours ready to strike back.

Squidgy's mind works like lightning. "This is not an auspicious start to my birthday. I can think of better ways to begin a celebration. I'll put off until tomorrow my journey around the Brook. I'll send Jacko off immediately to search for traces of Cajjer. I'll warn the SnuggleWump to not allow any visitors. Then I'll make myself a batch of Cornish splits to have with my elderberry wine at my birthday tea party. And I will be the only guest."

The thought is father to the action. "Home, Griselda, home!" She pushes the far end of her broomstick down with all her strength. The slowly ascending spiral suddenly turns into a corkscrew dive downwards. She pulls back desperately as the Brook zooms closer, levels out a few feet from the ground and careens in horizontal flight down the path to her cottage faster than any of the birds pursuing her.

She meets the third of the teros as it zooms upwards following the others. This tero makes a basic mistake, probably because she was once a chicken unaccustomed to the joys of sustained flight. The essence of streamlining is to close all openings to reduce wind resistance. This tero not only has a huge mouth, but she is flying with her mouth wide open, enjoying the cool breeze on her tonsils and her back teeth.

Mrs. Squidge pulls back hard on the broom handle as though it were a joystick. She attempts to fly over the tero, but the poor creature gets knocked so hard by the broom that her tiny brain can no longer function properly.

The tero, by its very design, is featherless. If it had been a normal-feathered bird, it would have filled the air with a flurry of feathers from the force of the impact. Its two tiny arms are so short that they are almost useless. They couldn't even carry a shopping basket. It does, however, have a mouthful of pointed teeth that are long enough to make a comb for a bear rug. Its mouth, like a crocodile's, makes up for its other deficiencies. As the titchy tero gets her open mouth jammed full to overflowing with twigs, she realizes too late the dangers of flying solo. The hapless tero bites down hard, cutting a huge swath through the twigs and succeeds in separating her mouthful of twigs from the broom.

Among the twigs in her mouth is the flagpole to which Vyruss, with renewed energy, is clinging to as hard as he can. This is his third ride so far this morning and he is still not yet anywhere near the farmhouse. He begins to question what he was told. "Has the wizard really carefully thought through all the details of this mission? It is in the small print that things tend to go wrong."

Even though the tero is little bigger than a blackbird, the flying trim of the broom has been seriously affected by the whacking great bite she took out of it. Probably no other single species of creature has as much mouth capacity as a pterodactyl. At least fifty percent of its body size can be accounted for by its mouth.

The broom falls backwards in a tumbling roll. Mrs. Squidge frantically works to get it back under control. It is not so crippled that it cannot fly, but its balance is seriously affected. It tilts sideways, and its lifting capacity is severely reduced. The fewer the twigs, the lesser the lift. The broom, pulled upwards by Mrs. Squidge, doesn't have the acceleration it had when she lifted off earlier in the day. It can't respond and droops sideways heading erratically towards the ground. It skids, bounces, and takes off again. Swinging crazily around the bend in the path, it careens between the two red lights of the SnuggleWump. Barely clearing the fence, it bounces on the porch and discharges Mrs. Squidge onto the floor of her living room. Crashing into the wall, it collapses into a messy heap. And so does Squidgy.

Mrs. Squidge gropes to her knees and crawls on all fours to push the door shut. She doesn't want any visitors just now.

Meanwhile, the tero, with her mouth full of twigs, is anxious only to catch up with the two teros who were ahead of her. She gains height and looks around. "Where are they? They've just disappeared!"

Behind her, Tuwhit and Rasputin encounter, head-on, the last three teros who were trying to imitate the maneuver of their sister ahead of them. Now the two larger birds and the three titchy teros are attempting to sort themselves out after their multiple midair collision. Feathers from the owl and the raven fill the air. Tuwhit and Rasputin, being experienced operators in free space, head for the safety of the open skies as mariners head for the open seas in a gale. They need to find a roost where they can rest and check the damage.

The three teros, being hens by nature, look for solid ground, but miss out. Following each other, they mistakenly believe the croc' pond is what they are looking for. It is covered with floating green weeds, and they assume it is a meadow. There are three splashes in quick succession.

This surprises Cajjer who is resting on the bank, trying to get his breath back. At the same time, he works at getting rid of the white flowers adorning his head like a fairy queen's wreath. The sudden splashes spur him into action, and he heads off lickety-split down the path towards the cottage. Taking a mighty leap between the two red lights, he twists in midair and bounces onto the porch. Without slowing down, he cracks his head a whacker on the door that he thought would still be wide open. He begins to think, *This is not one of my better days.*

Squidgy would agree. It has not been one of her better days either.

The Ambassador Arrives

Now soaring safely through the air in the mouth of the tero, the ambassador abandons the batwing idea. But Dr. Tyfuss recognizes that he can't just leave things to happen naturally. "What would the woodlouse leader do if he were in a situation like this? Well, for starters, he probably wouldn't find himself in a situation like this in the first place. Never mind, I need to influence events by taking the initiative and exercising leadership. Obviously, that is going to be difficult when I'm airborne high above the croc' pond, trying to hang on to the wrong end of a flagpole. The flag keeps wrapping itself around my head, and that is not the most favorable of circumstances. It didn't matter so much when it was dark except that I had trouble breathing when it was over my nose. But now that the first glimmer of light is appearing, it's a lot scarier." He takes a look down and is surprised at his location. "Given how long I've been airborne, I'm surprised I haven't traveled farther from the waterfall than I have."

He turns his gaze upwards and almost lets go of the flagpole. He has never before seen a tero. Woodlouses are not particularly attractive creatures, but they would win a beauty competition anywhere when matched against teros. Even the wizard gave a double take and almost swallowed his tonsils when he first saw one of them. Now Vyruss is even more scared than he was before. "The nearest thing to this vicious array of skin and bones and teeth must be a vampire bat coming in for the kill. This creature must be a Mouth. It is *all* mouth, and it's spitting out twigs like a combine harvester at full stretch consuming a wheat field. By comparison, a vampire bat is a cuddly toy for a restless baby."

Vyruss suddenly becomes very nervous. "There are only moments left before I am either spat out with the rest of the twigs or swallowed down as a gulped in-flight meal."

He shakes himself free from the flag once again wrapping itself around his head. "It would help if I had hold of the other end of the pole, but at this point, I have no idea how to get there. I wonder if I should let go of my pole and try a high dive into the pond? No, the wizard was insistent that when I arrive, I need to hold the black-and-white flag high. I'll have to try something else first."

The Mouth is intent on emptying itself of twigs as rapidly as possible. For Vyruss, the view is frightening. He swings his feet up, bends his legs at the top of the swing, and kicks down as hard as he can. He was trying to make himself into a small rocket. He fails miserably; his design is all wrong. However, his jerk does pull the end of his flagpole free from the twigs as they themselves are spat out into the air. His timing is perfect, although he can't claim any credit for what was, after all, an act of desperation. He is in freefall. What spurred his action was that he saw, ascending, but far beneath him, a duck. If he misses the duck, he is likely to have a wet landing in the croc' pond. But even if he does, there is still the chance he will survive.

He takes a closer look at the duck. He does not recognize it as a mallard. "Huh. It is bottle green, chocolate brown, and grey. It may not be white, but it is clearly a duck. It has a duck's bill and it quacks like a duck. As far as I'm concerned, a quack and a yellow bill means the bird is a duck no matter what color it is."

Far beneath the duck, Vyruss sees three more horrible creatures akin to the Mouth above. "Oh, no! They are diving into the croc' pond. There goes that option! The pond is clearly now out." He rethinks his plans. "Perhaps, if I can allow my hands to slide along the flagpole without going off the end, the flag will slow my descent. If I can avoid the duck's quacking bill, then I can taxi-glide into position for a soft landing on its back. But I dare not miss the duck and end up as fodder for the Mouths below.

"I wish I were free of the wizard's overcoat. If the worst happens and I have to swim for the shore, it's going to hamper me. On the other hand, if I hold my arms out wide as I descend, the coat may act as a parachute even if not wings. However, that would mean I'll be holding on to the flagpole with only one hand. There really are times when having four hands would be a distinct advantage." He floats free in the air, falling towards the duck directly below him.

The mallard, looking up, completely ignores Vyruss and his predicament as though he is not there. Instead, it gulps and does a double take on seeing the twig-spitting Mouth flying above him.

Vyruss notices the look of consternation on the duck's face. "I can't be sure what that duck is thinking, but I have a good idea. We are two minds with a single thought."

For a moment, the astounded bird actually stops flying. It considers, "Should I go up or down?" It quickly looks down to check. In the pond, he sees three minor volcanoes violently disturbing the waters. The three titchy pterodactyls cannot swim, and they look desperately for someone or something to cling on to. The duck is clearly sure. "It is not going to be me!" He looks up and is just as determined. "I'm not going in that direction either! I'm not keen to be made into minced duck patties. I may be bigger than the Mouth, but that's the only thing in my favor. The odds are too much." He is almost stationary while coming to the decision to tear off sharply sideways.

This is a perfect moment for an almost-parachutist from above. Vyruss, having successfully maneuvered to hold on to the flagpole by the correct end, lands on the duck's back facing the tail. He stumbles and grabs onto some feathers with his free hand. With a grateful sigh, he throws himself down. "For the first time since Rasputin collided with something in the dark, I'm not hanging on to the flag pole for dear life." He reminds himself, "In the future, I'll be sure to prepare for emergencies like this. I'll do a hundred push-ups a day to develop my arm muscles."

The duck is a local resident. In the sky over the Brook are friends and enemies. He knows who is who. Besides the three oddities in his pond and the one nearby spitting out twigs, there are two others like them in the distance towards Brook Lane. They appear to be approaching. Much closer in is a raven with a broken beak. These are the enemies.

Rasputin circles slowly at a safe distance and at the same height as the mallard. He watches the duck carefully as the daylight gains steadily over the darkness. He looks as though he is preparing to attack.

Around them, the strains of the dawn chorus are dying away, and the birds of the Brook begin to take their first foraging flights. These birds are friends. In an even closer circle, as though it is acting as guard against the raven, is an owl. The duck knows Tuwhit well. They are old friends and good acquaintances. Above, again circling slowly and looking down, is Crusty, the golden eagle that lives in the oak tree not far from the croc' pond. He is also a friend.

Tuwhit waggles his wings. It is a signal known to birds the world over. "Follow me." He flies slowly up the path from the croc' pond to the farmhouse.

The mallard follows. He realizes, 'There is something alive on my back. I don't know what it could be. It's not heavy enough to be a monster Mouth. It could be an injured bird needing a ride. I'll find out soon enough."

Crusty overflies the raven and follows the other two birds.

Rasputin circles the croc' pond once or twice before following a good distance behind. He relaxes more with every moment that passes. "Although things were hectic for a while, they seem to be working out according to plan." He stops in the May tree by the farm gate and gives a grateful sigh. "The ambassador is going to arrive right on time even though I haven't delivered him myself."

Tuwhit dips towards Uncle Andy's cow pond, indicating to the mallard that he can land there. But the bird does not need this easy landing and shakes his head. The owl leads him beside the top of the well in the farmhouse garden. The mallard lands easily and runs a few short paces forwards before he stops. He waits for his passenger to disembark. He is surprised at the little man who jumps off. He wonders, *Why is he swaddled in an overcoat on what promises to be a warm day? This is starting to be a day full of surprises.* He quacks uncertainly. Unsure where to go now, he rests for a while and then waddles over to Uncle Andy's pond. "I'll wait a while before I head back home."

It is not only the mallard who is surprised. Tuwhit, Crusty, and Jordy, who is on duty at Buffo's post while the toad is away with his choir, are all amazed to see who jumps to the ground.

Vyruss follows the wizard's instructions. He holds the black flag with the white circle in the center high above his head. He faces Jordy and yells out at the top of his voice: "PEACE. PEACE. I COME IN PEACE!" He catches his breath and shouts again, "PEACE. PEACE. I COME IN PEACE!"

Down at the gate, an attentive raven with a broken beak also hears the ambassador's shout and saunters into lazy flight towards Squidgy's cottage. "It's time to deliver the wizard's message to Mrs. Squidge. After that, I will be off to the waterfall and on towards the castle. All is well. The wizard's plan was perfect in every detail. What a master to work for! I can see in my mind's eye my master's pleasure when I report: 'Mission Completed.'

"And I know what he'll say. 'You're the only reliable servant I have. I knew I could depend on you, old fellow. If you want anything done right, give it to Rasputin, that's what I say. Well done, my lad! I wish I had a half dozen more like you.' I hope King Haymun is there to hear it. He seems to think that he is the big cheese at the castle."

"Peace. Peace. I Come in Peace!"

Vyruss has held his flag as high as he can and made his proclamation of peace at the top of his voice. *I'll be glad when I can take off this overcoat. It's getting warm already.* He has lost his hat. Unknown to him, it is floating on the surface of the empty croc' pond, brim down. If he ever gets it back, it is likely to be an even tighter fit. If he had it now, he would take it off and bow with a flourish towards Jordy whom he recognizes. He smoothes back his thick, brown, windblown hair in an attempt to make himself look more like an ambassador than a stunt man for a circus.

He finds and gently explores the extent of his bump and winces. He flexes the fingers on his left hand and then flexes them again. Hanging on to a flagpole while doing aerobatics locks them up, and it takes work to bring them back to normal. He wonders, *Will I ever again be able to put my signature on official documents so that people can recognize it?* Only Vyruss would be concerned about that. Other doctors deliberately scribble their names so no one can forge their signature. Still holding the flag high, he shifts it to his left hand so he can work on flexing the fingers of his right hand. They are tingling and feel almost numb.

Jordy is mystified. *Why did Vyruss give us such a strange greeting? Does the wizard have some secret plan? He must be up to something. Maybe he heard of the weddings on Friday and is out to spoil them or take advantage of the occasion for his own wickedness. Where did Vyruss get that overcoat? He wasn't wearing it when he left two weeks ago. It looks as though he is practicing to be a strangler. I had to flex my fingers like that once after being on a tug-of-war team. I frightened the umpire half to death doing that.*

Jordy is at the end of a long, but relaxed night watch. Things are really quiet on the Brook since the circus left. He leaps down the path to meet Vyruss. They are delighted to see each other. Joyfully, they embrace with the triple Twith hug. Somehow, they manage to avoid the flagpole. Jordy puts his arm around the doctor. "Greetings, my friend! You will surely have a story of adventures in Gyminge to tell us as soon as we gather everyone together. There must be an explanation for your odd arrival, but we can wait to find out about that."

Tuwhit and Crusty are also acquainted with the doctor. The last they knew, he was over in Gyminge. Crusty asks questions, but he doesn't really expect any answers from Tuwhit. "Where on earth has he suddenly come from? What was he doing flying around over the Brook clinging onto the side of Squidgy's broom? Why were they over the croc' pond? Where do the teros fit into the scheme of things?"

Tuwhit tells Crusty, "I'm heading back to the cottage. Rasputin is around, and where Rasputin is, the wizard is usually not far away. It is likely the wizard is back on the Brook. You need to inform Jock."

Vyruss wastes no time in small talk. He needs to get down to business. "I have returned, Jordy, my friend, but I am no longer merely a doctor and a secret ally. Things have very much changed since I left here a fortnight ago. I return with the authority of the Wizard of Wozzle to conduct negotiations with you on his behalf. Is Jock up yet? I have an urgent message for him."

"I don't know. It is just now dawn. Unless your yelling woke him up, he'll be asleep for a while yet. Is the message urgent enough to wake him up? Why did you shout out, 'Peace. Peace. I come in peace?' What kind of flag are you carrying? Where did you get it?"

"I'll tell you all in good time." Vyruss carries the flagpole over towards the entrance to Twith Mansion and sticks in the ground near the door that Buffo usually guards. The flag is limp and flutters half-heartedly. It is still damp and needs a stronger breeze.

Jordy unfurls the flag to full-size and looks at the large white circle of cloth on the black background curiously. He says nothing, but he is clearly thinking hard.

Barney is a light sleeper and appears at the door of Twith Mansion. He takes one puzzled look at the two men talking in front of him and disappears back down the passage as quickly as he appeared. As far as Barney is concerned, the arrival back of the captive who agreed to help them is reason enough to wake up the whole household. The boy proceeds to do so. Knocking loudly on the mansion bedroom doors, he wakens Jock, Gerald, Cydlo, Taymar, and Ambro, shouting, "Wake up! Dr. Tyfuss is back. He's got a flag." He bangs on the door of the three Shadow girls. "Ellie! Margaret! Ruthie! Wake up! The doctor is back!" Bimbo and Bollin have heard the ruckus and are already at their door.

Barney wastes no time in explaining. He is off up the passageway to the spiral staircase. Not pausing at the hearth, he continues on upstairs to bang on his sister's door and barges into his own bedroom that he shares with Stumpy. He shakes his uncle out of a deep sleep, dislodging the red sleeping cap with the bobble on top. "Uncle! Uncle! Dr. Tyfuss is back. He has a black-and-white flag and he yelled, 'Peace! Peace!' Come quickly!"

Cymbeline is in her nightgown; she hasn't taken time to pull on her bathrobe. She is into his bedroom and grabs Barney's shoulder. "Slow down, Barney. Slow down. Take a breath. Don't shout! Now tell us what is happening."

Elisheba, clad well enough for company, crowds behind her friend and passes her a bathrobe.

Stumpy sits up in bed. "Barney, tell us what you just saw. Who brought Dr. Tyfuss back? He couldn't get here by himself. Did Crusty or Tuwhit bring him?"

The boy is overly excited. "I don't know. I don't know. He's talking to Jordy outside. Come down and see. Come quickly. I'm sure something important has happened. Is there anything to eat?" His stomach responds to excitement with a feeling of imminent starvation, and he darts into the kitchen to scrounge around. The two girls head off downstairs. Stumpy shakes his head to try and get himself more awake and follows after them.

Barney wonders, *Should I wake up all the Beyonder children? If I do that though, I'll have to wait at the hearth to shrink them until they are all downstairs. I'll miss out on whatever's going on.* He decides, *I've already awakened all the people that it is really important to wake up. The others can find out later.* Stuffing the last of his bread and jam into his mouth, he darts downstairs after the others.

THE WIZARD'S MESSENGER

At the mansion entrance, Vyruss is warmly greeted by Bimbo and Bollin. The doctor has formed a friendship with these two Shadow boys when all three returned to Gyminge. He separated from them to assist the injured goblin king back to the castle. Later, Vyruss gave them timely warning to get back to the Brook before the tunnel was blocked by seven hundred and fifty returning goblins. They have little doubt of the doctor's loyalty.

For his part, Vyruss is pleased to see and welcome his two friends. As the Twith pour out of the mansion, he looks around. *I'm disappointed not to see the fair Cymbeline. Surely, there will be time to renew acquaintance later before I have to return to Gyminge.*

Still inside the mansion, Cydlo tells Jock, "As far as I can recall, I've never actually met Dr. Tyfuss. I know in the past he was King Haymun's personal physician. I did see him on occasion while delivering charcoal to the castle, so I know what he looks like. But I don't think he has ever seen me. When he was here before as a captive, you took precautions to have me stay out of sight while he was being interviewed."

Jock speaks gently, "Do ye think this may be th' time fur th' two o' ye ta mee'?"

The king is cautious. "Bring him in by all means, but let us first see what he has to say. I'll stay in my bedroom with the door ajar as I did the last time. We do not yet know whether he has played true or false. It will be better for Elisheba to stay upstairs until we know more about whose side he is actually on. We have been betrayed before. Ambro should also stay out of sight for a while."

Jock asks Ellie, "Will ye go warn Elisheba ta remain upstairs? I'll go tell Ambro ta stay out o' sigh'." He lets Ambro know, "Ye cun leave th' door ajar so tha' ye cun 'ear wha' th' doctor 'as ta say." He goes out to greet Vyruss.

The new ambassador is glad to see Jock. As they share hugs, Vyruss whispers, "I have an urgent message just for you."

Jock nods acknowledgment. Like Jordy, he looks with curiosity at the flag Vyruss brought with him. He stretches it out to full-size to observe it better. He tells Jordy, "Please remain on guard duty 'til I cun send sumone ta take yur place. Thanks. Cum on, Vyruss, le's go inside."

Vyruss hangs up his overcoat in the passage and continues to flex his fingers and knuckles. They are still quite sore.

Cymbeline, Stumpy, and Barney arrive from upstairs. As Cymbeline comes in to join the others, Vyruss thinks, *The girl seems to turn up the brightness of the lighting as she enters the room. I'm pleased I'm wearing my best formal suit. I wish I'd had time to wash my face and comb my hair.* He stands a little straighter and makes a conscious effort to stop flexing his knuckles.

Cymbeline flashes a smile of greeting to the tired traveler that renews his energy. She looks around for Ambro and tries to hide her disappointment when she doesn't see him. Taymar whispers to her why Ambro isn't present, so she relaxes a bit.

Jock asks Barney, "Will ye run back up ta th' attic 'n' git one o' th' boys ta cum down 'n' replace Jordy?"

Barney races away. He doesn't want to be gone too long. Micah, the energetic grandson from Washington, is already awake and offers to relieve Jordy of guard duty. He always wakes up hungry. *I could sure do with a slice of bread smothered with peanut butter and bacon bits.* Micah likes bacon on anything and everything—even ice cream.

Ellie has rejoined the other Shadow girls, and they scurry around the kitchen working on an early breakfast. Ruthie cooks the porridge and sees to the boiled eggs. Margaret slices the bread and places it on the table along with the butter and jam. She also fills glasses with juice or milk. Ellie brews the tea and sets the table.

Cymbeline takes charge for a moment. "Jock, we will all want to hear what the doctor has to tell us about his adventures. I suggest no talking about that until we have had a quick breakfast, cleared the table, and stacked the dirty dishes. Then we will have time to pay full attention to what he has to say and no one will miss out. Can Dr. Tyfuss wait that long?"

The doctor answers for himself. "I think that's a grand idea. I have had a busy night and would like to tidy myself up a little. Traveling takes it out of a person. I could do that while the breakfast is being prepared. Where can I do that?"

Jock nods agreement to Cymbeline's proposal and leads Vyruss to his own bedroom. Jordy is not yet back in. Vyruss takes the opportunity to push the door almost closed and whispers urgently. "Jock, I am on an errand from the wizard. He appointed me as his ambassador to negotiate with you. He told me I have to tell you only the truth in order that you will believe me. What I have to say is urgent. He wants me to be back in Gyminge by noon with your answer to his proposal. Can you arrange that for me? Also, when I tell what's been happening, can I speak freely or should I wait until later when we can be alone?"

"We 'ave no secrets frum each other, Vyruss. If ye say anythin' tha' is better nay said, I will interrupt ye. Bu' 'til then go righ' a'ead 'n' share e'erythin' quite freely. I'll git ye a clean towel, and leave ye now so ye cun tidy yurself up."

Micah has carried Barney down from the attic, out the front door of the farmhouse, around to Twith Mansion, and sets him on the ground next to Jordy.

Jordy warns him, "Be very alert and don't stray from your post. Crusty says Rasputin is back on the Brook so the wizard won't be far away." He and Barney disappear into Twith Mansion.

Jock meets the two returning Twith as he leaves his bedroom and tells Jordy, "Do nay turn in yet. Vyruss is in thur righ' now, 'n' thur is goin' ta be an early breakfas'. After tha', 'e 'as a message fur us frum th' wizard. Ye will surely wan' ta be presen' fur tha'." He turns towards Cydlo's bedroom and pauses with his hand on the handle. "Barney, I 'ave another errand fur ye. Run back upstairs agin 'n' tell Gumpa 'n' gran'ma wha' is 'appenin'. They'll be drinkin' tea in bed, so they'll be awake. Take th' rollin' pin ta bang on th' door. Keep on bangin' 'til they open i'. Tell them Vyruss says 'e 'as a message frum th' wizard fur us. Ask if they wuld like ta join us. They cun cum down in 'bout twenty minutes. Breakfas' shuld be ready by then. Ye won't need ta stay ta shrink them, ye cun ask Elisheba ta do tha' fur ye. 'Urry!"

Barney enjoys being the messenger at such an exciting time. *This is why the world just couldn't manage without boys! It would just collapse into a crumpled cube. Boys like myself make the best telegram carriers, the best errand boys, the best newspaper boys, the best helpers to the milk and bread deliverymen, and the best pizza delivery boys too. We have energy to burn. Girls don't have as much energy as boys. When you light a girl's energy, it burns like a tiny candle flame. When you light a boy's energy, stand well back! You have started a bonfire!*

Barney bangs hard on Gumpa's bedroom door. It is not only Gumpa and gran'ma who hear it; the racket wakes the entire household. Children pour from all the bedrooms. Even Elisheba hurries out to see what the commotion is. "What's going on?"

"Jock wants Gumpa and gran'ma down in Twith Mansion right away. Will you shrink them for me? Thanks." He scurries back downstairs. He is determined not to miss anything.

Gran'ma asks Stormy, "Will you take charge of the breakfast preparations for me? I may be delayed, and I don't want the children going hungry."

Stormy readily fills in for gran'ma. Those who are up early lend a hand.

Elisheba sits on the top of the microwave, watching what is going on. She tells Ginger, "There is an unexpected visitor from Gyminge down in Twith Mansion. A conference is going on that must not be interrupted. I'm not even allowed to be part of it. I wish that applied to Taymar as well. We still have so much to talk about."

Ginger smiles sympathetically. "Well, you just stay with us until it's over. I'm sure they'll be up to get you soon."

Stormy and her crew have breakfast ready. The bell is rung and the children scurry to the tables. Without Gumpa present, Specs fills in to say grace. There seems to be an attempt, at least by the boys, to clear everything edible off both tables. Lucas, a grandson from Washington, eats as though this will be his last chance to have any food before the wedding feast next Friday. He feels that because boys were given greater appetites than girls, it is boys who should be given the right to empty the plates of edibles. Ginger is not alone in disputing his claims. Stormy organizes the washing and cleanup squads. Specs announces, "There will be an inspection of all the bedrooms except Gumpa's and gran'ma's." The children manage well on their own and do not miss the grownups at all.

DR. TYFUSS REPORTS

The Little People gather into the large room of Twith Mansion. It is good that the table Stumpy and Jordy made years ago when they first moved in is as big as it is. Even so, it is hardly big enough. Already seated are the seven original Twith, the five Shadow children, and Dr. Tyfuss. Two others, unseen, are listening carefully behind bedroom doors left slightly ajar. Gumpa and gran'ma join the others at the breakfast table. They dressed in a hurry and carried Elisheba downstairs to shrink them. They both greet the stranger. Gumpa, who has not met him before, introduces gran'ma and himself.

Jock addresses Gumpa, "Will ye say grace fur us? We'll wai' ta 'ear wha' Vyruss 'as ta say 'til after we finish our meal."

The delicious breakfast is quickly consumed with little conversation. Everyone is anxious to hear what the doctor has to say. Even Gumpa, who is a slowpoke at eating, finishes the same time as everyone else. The kitchen worktops are stacked with the clutter of breakfast cooking pots and pans, dirty dishes, and cutlery. Cymbeline keeps her promise to leave the cleanup until later. Gumpa observes the kitchen mess with approval, while gran'ma grimaces and looks the other way. She always prefers to get the kitchen tidy immediately. They settle down to listen.

The two Beyonders recognize that there is little doubt that Dr. Vyruss Tyfuss is a Twith, not a goblin. Whatever the wizard did to the other citizens of Gyminge to change them into goblins, it did not happen to this man. He appears ready to smile. There is a sparkle in his eyes and an openness to his face. He, alone among them, wears a formal black suit and a necktie. Gran'ma thinks, *He does not look frightened like the goblins that I saw in the castle. In fact, he looks quite at ease.* She finds herself prepared to like him.

Gumpa is still checking whether there is a twitch anywhere, but does not detect one.

Jock sits next to the doctor. "Welcum ta ye all. We 'ave an unexpected surprise in th' arrival earlier this mornin' o' Dr. Vyruss Tyfuss back frum Gyminge. Th' good doctor was physician ta th' goblin king. Like us, 'e wishes ta 'elp 'is country back ta freedom. 'E freely agreed ta return ta Gyminge ta 'elp us. This put 'im a' considerable personal risk. 'E went off with Bimbo 'n' Bollin jus' two weeks ago. 'E separated frum th' boys ta stay with th' goblin king who was injured. We know little more 'bout 'is experiences since then. Per'aps ye wuld like ta take up th' story, Vyruss. Our time is unlimited, bu' ye may nay 'ave tha' much time ta share e'erythin'."

Vyruss nods a smile and is quick to respond. "I'll need to cut the earlier part of my story short. To begin with, let me just say that when I went back to Gyminge, I expected great difficulty because of what I agreed to do. You here are accustomed to always telling the truth. Jock explained to me the importance of doing that at all times. I was willing to accept the challenge, and while I was with you, it became quite easy. However, I anticipated far greater trouble once I was back in Gyminge where the circumstances are very different. Then I would be under the authority of either King Haymun or the wizard. I would have said that it is not possible to survive without lying in our world of Gyminge. To my great surprise, I found that it gets easier as time passes. Silence is a great substitute for false speech. I find that it can actually give an impression of inner wisdom that I do not actually possess."

He smiles wryly, and the others all grin as well. "I have discovered that a lie takes place in the mind before it is ever spoken. If the mind is clear of deceit, the lie does not occur. By always speaking the truth, I find that I sleep better. Can you imagine that?"

Twith and Beyonders alike don't have to imagine it. They know it is true. Heads nod around the room.

"Another benefit is that I no longer have to pause and consider what answer to give to any questions I might be asked. Even though the wizard has total power to harm me, I am contented and relaxed.

"The king relieved me of my position as his personal physician and appointed me to construct a fort just inside Gyminge at the southern border. He called it an immigration control center where all immigrants, including toads, would be questioned. If necessary, they would be required to return to the Brook." He laughs out loud. "That doesn't seem likely to me."

This time, heads shake back and forth, and the broad smiles on every face indicate that the listeners don't think so either.

"I was engaged in that work last Sunday when I received a personal message from the Wizard of Wozzle to hand over my work to Major Bubblewick, return to the castle immediately, and report to him no later than noon the following day. That order made me quite fearful. I thought that my agreement to work with you had been discovered, and I expected to be severely punished. However, that was not what happened. He treated me cordially, even with friendship, and explained that he had an important assignment for me over here on the Brook. He asked me to volunteer for reassignment as Ambassador of Gyminge to the Beyond for an indefinite length of time. I did not find it necessary to explain to him that I had previously visited the Brook, although King Haymun is well aware of that. Fortunately, they do not appear to be talking at present, so as far as I know, the wizard knows nothing of my experiences on this side of the border. King Haymun, even though he lives in the apartments right next to the wizard, was excluded from all our conversations. The wizard said that the king was indisposed, but I think that was most likely untrue and he had been deliberately excluded from our meetings.

"The wizard explained that, for reasons of State, it was essential that the Twith hand over to him the Twith Book of Lore without trickery. It must be the complete Book of Lore with no omissions or alterations. Because this would require delicate negotiations, he instructed me to tell you the truth at all times. He gave me complete liberty to explain all that would be happening in his apartments, and that what I was about to see could be shared in full detail with you. He had no concerns about letting me do that and even encouraged me to tell you absolutely everything."

Gerald is anxious to catch every word. As he tips his head and leans forward, his blond ponytail flips over his shoulder. He brushes it back. *It is clear that the wizard didn't know when he stole it, that it was a pseudo Book of Lore containing Gumpa's Cornish recipes. He took it back to Gyminge on Saturday. Either that same day or the next, he discovered it is not what he thought. He is responding quickly. The wizard's reaction is to use truth itself against us to trick us into giving up the authentic Book of Lore.* Gerald shudders.

Cydlo is up from his chair and looks through the narrow slit of his door hinges as close as he can get without being seen. He also shudders. *This desperate move of the wizard to use truth against us means he will stop at nothing to secure his ends.*

The only sound in the room is the doctor's voice. "The wizard told me that a group of interfering Beyonders live in the farmhouse, and he intends to teach them a lesson. He said that here among you is the old king of Gyminge, King Rufus. I knew nothing about that. On behalf of the wizard, I am authorized to make a proposal to the king, but only to the king and no one other than the king. It is for the mutual benefit of both the king and the wizard. He was certain you would agree. This is the purpose of my appointment—to bring the proposal here and present it to the king. Then I am to return with your response. I was given a deadline to be back at the border fort by noon today."

The Little People betray their concern at this news. Gerald wonders, *How did the wizard find out that King Rufus is among us? Certainly, it can't be the doctor. We didn't discover that Cydlo is the king until after Vyruss left with Bollin and Bimbo to return to*

Gyminge. Where has our security broken down? None of our ene-mies—Jacko, Mrs. Squidge, Cajjer, or even Rasputin—can possibly know. The pseudo Book of Lore was taken under circumstances we haven't been able to explain, and now there's been a leak that the king is here.

Gumpa has a question. "Tell us, Dr. Tyfuss, just where are the wizard and Rasputin at this time?"

"Oh, I can tell you that. The wizard plans to leave the castle in Gyminge in about another hour. He will go to the southern border on horseback. He should arrive there by late afternoon. I cannot tell you quite where Rasputin is just now. He was in the process of getting me across the bog when he collided with something that wrenched me out of his claws. I ended up wedged in the twigs of the old woman's broomstick. Wherever he is now, he will be back at the southern border by noon. I am to let him know the king's response to the proposal I am to give him. He will take that news to the wizard wherever he may happen to be along his journey."

THE KING AND THE RING

Vyruss has the attention of everyone present. He continues, "Before I present the proposal, I have two things I need to do first. If the king is indeed here, I need to present him with the credentials the wizard gave me to prove I am the official Ambassador of Gyminge to the Beyond. In order that I may negotiate and speak on his behalf, the king must approve my credentials. If the king is not here, then I may not present the proposal. I am to return to Gyminge and tell the wizard that the king is not here.

"I also have a personal and private letter for the king from a person I am not allowed to name. I promised the writer that I would deliver this letter into the hands of the king and to no one else. If it cannot be delivered, I will return the letter, unopened to her."

Cydlo is startled into action at the mention of a woman. He has heard enough. *It is up to me now, not Jock. The wizard is throwing down the gauntlet to me.* Clad only in his pajamas and bathrobe, he is not yet dressed and ready for the day. His red hair is unruly, but he doesn't let that stop him. He steps out from behind the bedroom door.

Gerald rises from his seat and offers it to Cydlo. Without a word of explanation, he disappears quickly into his office.

Vyruss rises from his own chair in surprise and respect. *So! It is true what the wizard told me. But is this truly the king or just an impostor? Obviously, from the reaction of the other Twith, they believe him to be the king.*

Cydlo accepts Gerald's chair with a smile and a nod of his head. Jordy brings another chair to the table for when the High Seer returns. The others shuffle chairs to make room for it. The king makes no attempt to introduce himself, and the others await developments in silence.

Vyruss is respectful and apologetic. He addresses Cydlo. "Sir, I speak with respect, but I do not know for certain that you are the king. You certainly resemble what I remember of him. I would like to believe that you are the king, but I believed that King Rufus died long ago. However, I have given my word to two people that the letters they sent with me will be handed over to the king and no one else. I will keep that word as far as I am able. Can you please confirm to me that you are King Rufus himself and not someone who happens to resemble him?"

Those around the table are silent. They are trying to make sense of the doctor's remark that he carries a private letter written to the king by a woman. *Which woman? Could it be Pru or Nettie?*

It is Gerald who breaks the silence. He has returned and holds up for all to see a ring. The wide gold band is made to fit a large finger. It holds a huge single ruby, artfully cut, in the center and smaller stones set on each side in the filigree band. "Dr. Tyfuss, kindly look at this ring that I hold in my hand. I place it on my finger, so! The tradition of the Twith is that when the king—and only when the king of Gyminge—wears this ring, it will glow with an inner light of its own. Jock, will you place it on your finger and then pass it to Jordy to do the same? Then Cydlo can try it and pass it on to the next if that proves necessary."

Vyruss has caught the name Cydlo. *Clearly, this is the man that the wizard spotted last Saturday while on State business in the farmhouse. The wizard believes he is King Rufus. But is he?*

Jock takes the ring from Gerald and tries it on. It is loose on his finger. He displays the ring to the table of watchers. Jordy does the same. He passes it to Cydlo.

Cydlo's hand is not the manicured hand of a courtier. It is a roughened, working man's hand with broad fingers bruised and thickened by toil. The man behind the hand wears no kingly garb, but only a secondhand dressing gown. Even though the ring has a large diameter, it fits tightly on Cydlo's ring finger. All eyes are now focused on the ring.

As soon as the ring is positioned on Cydlo's finger, it begins to glow with a warm, red light. It gains strength from within itself as though merely slipping it on his finger turned on some electric switch. The radiant, red glow continues to gleam brighter and brighter. The whole room is bathed in rich, soft, red light streaming from the ring. The light from the ring, though ruby red, is brighter than the light in the room.

Cydlo slips off the ring, and the ruby red light fades. He returns it to Gerald who goes to put it away where it is kept hidden. No one wants to say anything until Gerald resumes his place. All of them, including Vyruss, have a sense of awe and wonder.

Vyruss breaks the silence. "Sire, may I present my credentials as Ambassador of Gyminge to the Beyond. If you will accept these, I am in a position to speak on behalf of the wizard."

Cydlo takes the small envelope, examines the seal with interest, sighs, breaks the seal, and opens the envelope. It is a formal, State letter, purporting to come from Gyminge Castle, informing that the bearer, Dr. Vyruss Tyfuss, is the duly authorized Ambassador of Gyminge to the Beyond appointed by the State of Gyminge and is entitled to make representations on behalf of the Wizard of Wozzle. It is written in a flourishing hand and signed by the wizard with a similar flourish. Cydlo nods his acceptance and places the letter to one side on the table in front of him. "Proceed, Mr. Ambassador."

"Sire, I wish to tell you what I observed in the castle at Gyminge on Monday. Responding to orders I received, I arrived there from the southern border at noon. The wizard informed me of my assignment as Ambassador of Gyminge to the Beyond. He then cleared all servants from the large hall in his apartments and gave strict orders that we were not to be interrupted.

"He explained that when the north lake was enlarged to encircle the castle, an escape tunnel was revealed and destroyed. The far end emerged into a distant quarry, but the end within the castle began in the very room where we were meeting. The wizard had the tunnel blocked at the first landing of the steps descending into the lake, but he retained the secret room for his own private use.

"He went to the fireplace and pulled a lever that I could not see. The back of the fireplace swung aside in an arc to the left-hand side without noise and exposed behind it a hideaway room about the size of a small bedroom. We went inside. I could see where a flight of steps once descended to the outside, but the exit is now completely blocked off by a stone wall. The wizard pointed out a spy-hole back into the great hall.

"What completely caught my attention was a pair of low wooden trestles on which rested something like a coffin covered with a very dusty, plain green cloth. I knew what it was at once. It had to be one of those green bottles the wizard keeps his enemies in. I was sure that the wizard was playing a wicked game, toying with me as a cat plays with a mouse. I was sure I would be the one to occupy the bottle. There was no hope of escape."

THE WOMAN IN
THE BOTTLE

Everyone listens to what Vyruss says with complete attention. Their minds are filled with strange surmise. Ambro, having been bottled himself, is particularly interested. *I can see that the doctor's fears for himself were unfounded for he is sitting here now. Who could be in the bottle? Surely, that must be the point of his story. I feel sorry for whoever it is. I suppose Taymar, Gerald, the king, and myself are the ones most likely to be acquainted with someone who was bottled. It could be anyone from the past.*

Vyruss continues, "I had no need to be fearful. It seems the wizard has, at least as far as I am concerned, turned over a new leaf. For the moment anyway, he is allowing truth to govern his actions. I have no need to fashion lies into the story. He wants you to trust me. Only in that way can his plans come to pass.

"The wizard asked me to help him lift the dusty, cloth-covered coffin over to a long, low table set close by. We did so. Its weight confirmed there was someone inside. As you can well imagine, I was relieved the bottle was not empty.

"The wizard wanted no mess on the floor to betray to the servants what we were doing. We rolled back the dusty cloth with great care. I carried it back into the room to get it out of the way. He dusted the bottle clean. It was not possible to make out through the glass who the person inside could be. The wizard used a poker to clean off the wax that sealed the plug tight. The wax came away easily and was dumped onto the dust cloth. I could see that this particular plug had two pull handles so that it would release smoothly. I held tight to the bottom of the bottle while the wizard pulled. At first, the plug gave, but only slightly, and then it suddenly came free. When it released, there was a loud pop. The dust cloth and the gathered wax was also stashed in the hideaway room.

"It was time to release whoever was in the bottle. The wizard tapped on the bottle to wake the person up. He told me to continue doing it while he yelled into the mouth of the bottle. That sound must have echoed around inside for whoever was sleeping was awakened. The wizard called out, 'Reach up and hold on to my hands.' His arms were inside the bottle as far as they would go. I put my arms around the wizard's waist and gave a heave. Fortunately, the bottle did not slip on the table.

"All three of us fell back onto the floor in a heap. When we picked ourselves up and sorted ourselves out, I discovered, to my immense surprise, that the bottle had yielded up a woman!"

Vyruss enjoys telling his story. Everyone around the table is fascinated with what he is saying. He knows, *They are desperate to know who the woman is that suddenly emerged into the story. But a good storyteller tries to keep the surprise from the listener's understanding as long as possible. For this limited time, they are captives in my hand and will have to wait.*

He smiles and feeds them a little more information to whet their appetites. "The woman was unsteady on her feet. She was slender in build and wore a plain, grey homespun blouse and skirt down to her ankles. She looked like a peasant woman. In age, she was somewhere between Cymbeline and gran'ma, but it was hard at first to tell quite where. Her long, light brown hair was tied back from her face, which was quite pale and drawn, showing her long captivity.

"We helped her to the nearby chair. She had some difficulty walking. We gave her water to drink. She appeared to be frightened, especially as she looked at and recognized the wizard. I didn't know who she was, but she wasn't afraid of me. In fact, later, she directed her questions to me instead of the wizard. She rubbed and blinked her eyes and stretched and wriggled her body as she eased back into the chair. Movement was becoming easier. She swallowed hard and cleared her throat. In a quiet voice, she asked us who we were, what was happening, and what time it was.

"Her voice surprised me. It was not a countrywoman's voice but the voice of someone who is well educated and well read. The wizard was being as kind and considerate as he could be and answered her questions gently. He didn't want to frighten her. He showed her where she might freshen herself up. While she was engaged in that, we replaced the bottle in the hideaway room and closed it up. We tidied the main room so that the servants would not know that anything had happened, except that from somewhere mysterious, a woman had come to visit us. I don't know what answer the servants found to that question.

"The wizard explained to the woman that he did not expect her to remain long at the castle, but that while she was his guest, she would be treated kindly. She would be housed in one of the State apartments, although she would not be at liberty to wander around the castle. She would also be given a maidservant who happens to be deaf and dumb.

"The woman asked me who I was and what I was doing in this particular situation. I replied that I had just been appointed to take a message to King Rufus in the Beyond, that I planned to leave the castle the following morning. I did not yet know what that message was. I offered to carry a letter to the king for her also, giving her my solemn promise that once she delivered it to me, it would either be delivered to the king or I would personally return it to her unopened. The wizard was in agreement.

"Yesterday morning, just as I was leaving the castle to begin my journey south, she handed me a letter. It has not been out of my possession since I received it from her. No one at all except myself has had access to it. It is sealed and initialed by her and the seal can be examined to verify that it has not been broken.

"I am satisfied, Sire, that she intended this letter to be delivered to you. I will be grateful if you will examine the seal carefully and satisfy yourself that neither the seal nor the envelope has in any way been tampered with."

Vyruss reaches into his inside pocket. There are two letters still inside, but the queen's letter is thick and readily selected. He removes it, checks that it is addressed to 'King Rufus, by hand.' He rises from his chair, walks around to Cydlo, and hands it to him.

THE LETTERS

As the ambassador returns to his chair and sits down, all eyes are on Cydlo.

The king glances down at the brown envelope in his hands. He did not know what to expect, but it is not this! He recognizes, with a shock like an arrow through his heart, the handwriting. He flinches and closes his eyes and the pain comes flooding back in. Although it is more than a thousand years, he remembers, as though it were yesterday, the last time he saw the writer. Some memories are eternal. The long, long years without her in the woodcutter's cottage seemed like an eternity. *What awful trick is the wizard playing now? Does his wickedness have no limits? Is nothing sacred?*

Tears well up inside him, preparing to be a flood that will soon engulf him. He cannot speak. His world is in turmoil. Forcing a smile towards the others, he pushes back his chair and almost stumbles to his bedroom. He pushes the door closed, throws himself on his bed, and sobs as though his heart would break. Pictures of the last time he saw her crowd through his mind. *I assured her then that everything would be all right, and it hadn't been. She didn't want to leave me, and I urged her on her way to stay with Alicia at the cottage hidden in the forest. I could never forgive myself for what happened to her. If I had sent more men with her to guard her or if I had kept her with me, everything could have been so different.* He continues to sob heavily. It is as though the tears somehow purge the pain of his past and must flow until that is accomplished.

For a while, those outside listening to the distress within the bedroom do not stir from their places around the table. Cymbeline wants to go to Elisheba. Jock half rises to go to the king, but gran'ma raises her hand to stay him. "Let him be, Jock. It is necessary for him to be alone just now. Let's just wait for him to come back. He will return when he has worked through the pain and is able to continue. He knows we are here and will still be here when he is ready. He'll not leave unfinished business. Cymbeline, maybe you girls can make a pot of tea. I think we all need a cup. Do it quietly, though. Vyruss, you haven't told us how you got here this morning Did you have any difficulty?"

Vyruss knows that he must wait until the king absorbs the contents of his wife's letter. It is likely to take some while. This will be an opportunity to share this morning's misadventures. He smiles wryly. "Well, I almost didn't make it. My knuckles are still sore. I'm not sure you're interested in all the details."

Gerald is curious to know why Vyruss arrived with such an odd flag and interrupts him. "Could you first tell us about the flag you brought? It has a peculiar design."

"The wizard had it made especially for me to bring to you. He said that it would ensure that I got a first hearing with you. If I hadn't had to carry the flag, the trip might not have been quite so terrible."

"Why did the wizard say that about the flag? Can you remember the actual words he used? This is important."

"It was not long after I arrived. I was really hungry. I'd traveled a long distance. The stewards brought tea and hazelnut biscuits, but no lunch. A servant brought in the flag and the wizard inspected it carefully. He satisfied himself that the white circle was sewn on neatly and firmly. If I remember correctly, when he gave me instructions, he said something like: 'Listen carefully. I have good reason to believe that the rebels expect a messenger with a black-and-white flag. You may be a stranger to them, but the flag you carry will be your authority. A surrender flag would be all white, but this is a negotiating flag I am sending. They will not question you. They may even be expecting you. Raise your flag high above your head as soon as you see one of them. Call out loudly, Peace. Peace. I come in peace!' That's why I did what I did when I arrived this morning, so that I could later tell the wizard I did exactly as he said."

Gerald becomes anxious. "This is disturbing news! What caused the wizard to believe we expect a messenger with a black-and-white flag? The only possible reference I can think of to a black-and-white flag is in Dayko's Rime itself. We'll talk about this later among ourselves. What you don't know about, Vyruss, you can't be tricked into passing on to the wizard. I'm quite worried about the apparent steady leakage of information to the wizard. How is it happening? None of us is a spy for the wizard. That is unthinkable!"

Vyruss continues with his story of the morning's adventures. It becomes clear there have been a series of near disasters. The mallard's delivery of the ambassador escorted by Crusty and Tuwhit was never even remotely a part of the wizard's planning.

While he talks, all of them have their ears cocked towards the bedroom. The sobbing lapses into silence. A while later, there are sounds of movement from within. The door opens and the king, now washed, combed, and fully dressed, emerges. His eyes are red rimmed, but strangely, he is smiling. He quietly resumes his place at the table.

Cymbeline pours him a cup of tea and refills several other cups.

Cydlo takes a first drink and looks around. "Friends, for what just happened, I beg your indulgence. I received unexpected news that caught me by surprise, but it was not news that can be considered bad. More of that later. Mr. Ambassador, you delivered a letter to me according to your promise to a lady. You told us there is yet another letter."

"Yes, Sire. I was shown this letter yesterday morning before I departed from Goblin Castle so I know its contents. The letter is sealed and addressed to you in the wizard's hand. He suggested that I read it to you and to whoever else might be present. Then I am to respond to any questions you might have about its contents. After that, I should leave you to formulate any reply you might wish me to take back to him. If there is a bed somewhere where I might rest, that would suit me well. I've had a strenuous night. However, I would like to leave shortly after eleven, so could you please wake me—if I'm not up?" Vyruss removes from his inner pocket the second letter, and this one he passes down to the king rather than delivering it by hand.

The king looks carefully at both the envelope and the seal. The wizard has addressed it: *King Rufus, by hand, Private, personal, and confidential.* He pauses a moment and then breaks the seal and removes the letter. He reads it slowly, concentrating carefully on what he reads. He is obviously deep in thought. No one else moves. He slips the letter back into its envelope and passes it back along to Vyruss. "Mr. Ambassador, I think the wizard's counsel was right. Would you please be good enough to read the letter out loud to all of us?"

The Wizard's Proposal

Vyruss removes the letter from the envelope, taking a long slow look around the table. The king's face is as impassive as he can make it, but within, he is in turmoil. He will wait and observe responses.

Respected King Rufus,

I must first of all congratulate you upon your survival! I had fondly believed that you had died of your wounds somewhere in the Beyond, but if not, I will be grateful that was not so. It makes possible and advisable this letter.

We are enemies of each other, and that is a situation unlikely to change. Sometimes, even enemies find it wise to pause and talk. I have something I wish to discuss with you and propose a short truce between us until, say, Wednesday evening. I undertake to commit no acts of hostility or even espionage against you until then. I trust you may feel able to respond in a similar way.

My subject is the Book of Lore. You tricked me once, and that is once too many for I am a proud man. I have tried to obtain it by traditional methods, but I have not succeeded.

I want the Book of Lore. And I want the real, complete, original, and unaltered Book of Lore. I want the one that your companions took from Dayko's house the day he fell.

As you know, I suffer from an unfortunate malady known as The Magician's Twitch. This causes me much discomfort and I wish to be rid of it. I understand that within the Lore of the Twith is an ancient remedy for this affliction that is unfailingly effective. I want it. You have it. If you do not have it, then say so and I will accept your word.

However, if you do have the original, real, and unchanged Book of Lore, AND it does indeed contain the remedy for the

Magician's Twitch, then I am willing to make an exchange for it.

I offer in exchange for the Book of Lore the person of Queen Sheba, your wife, alive, in good health, and well treated. I shall be saddened to lose the pleasure of her company, but no doubt, she will be pleased with the alternative.

I offer no trickery, only a fair exchange. You can test my ambassador by questioning him carefully. He has my instructions to answer all your questions as truthfully as he can. I have placed no restraints upon him.

My proposal, if you agree, is that we make the exchange at a point you select on the border between Gyminge and the Brook. Set a place and a time and the queen and I will be there on the Gyminge side.

I have communicated the actual procedure for the exchange to my ambassador. I shall not try to trick you, and expect that you will not try to trick me.

I suggest the exchange take place the afternoon of Wednesday before the end of our truce in order that we do not surprise each other with unpleasantness.

I request that you facilitate the return of my ambassador to the waterfall entrance to the kingdom in order that he may communicate your response to me.

If your response is agreement to my proposal, you can expect him back within the hour after dropping him off.

Sincerely, Griswold Beswetherick-Jacka

As Vyruss reads, startled gasps of astonishment occasionally escape from open mouths. Excited glances flash back and forth, but no words are exchanged.

The king addresses the ambassador. "Before we consider this proposal, Mr. Ambassador, kindly advise us of the exact manner of the exchange proposed. When you have done so, we will discuss the proposal among ourselves. I am sure Jock can arrange a place for you to rest as we do so. You will have our answer to take back to Gyminge before eleven."

"Sire, I trust I won't forget anything important. The wizard advised me that the exchange could take place as early as teatime today if matters move along rapidly. From his side, he will be ready. He is already traveling by horse with the queen and an escort from the castle to the southern border. Rasputin will meet me within Gyminge at noon and I will give him your response. If you have agreed, I will tell him the time and the place you propose for the rendezvous. He will then locate the wizard in his journey, and I will return to you on the Brook. I am to act as your hostage.

"The wizard will be present on the Gyminge side with the queen at the time and place you set. On the Brook side, I will satisfy myself that what you offer in the exchange is indeed the genuine Book of Lore. I will expect you, Sire, and also Jock and Gerald to affirm it is the true and complete Lore, and that it has not been altered. We must verify that it does indeed contain the cure for The Magician's Twitch.

"The queen and the Book of Lore will be exchanged simultaneously. The Book of Lore is to be placed in a protective waterproof bag and given to me. Together, the king and I will place it on the ground as close to the curtain as we can get. We will then both withdraw forty paces.

"The wizard will not be disguised and will be at least forty paces distant from the curtain on the Gyminge side. No one else watching either from Gyminge or from the Brook shall be nearer than one hundred paces.

"The queen will come forward and present herself alone at the curtain at the same spot where the Book of Lore is. When she has done so, and you, Sire, have affirmed she is indeed the queen, then I will approach the curtain alone. You, Sire, will remain where you are. I will pick up the Book of Lore and stand facing the queen with only the curtain between us.

"Once the wizard is satisfied that you are not playing any tricks, he will briefly open a pair of slits in the curtain. This will allow me, with the Book of Lore, and the queen to pass each other as we step through to the other side. As soon as this happens, the curtain will be sealed again and the agreed transaction will be completed. Are there any questions?"

The Ambassador
Takes a Nap

The Twith have many questions for the ambassador. "Do you think that the wizard can be trusted in this proposal or is it another of his tricks?"

"Actually, I do think he can be trusted this time. I think the wizard realizes that he hasn't been successful in obtaining the Book of Lore by unfair means, so now he is trying fair means."

Cydlo has a question of his own. "Do you think it was really Queen Sheba you met?"

"Yes, I do. However, I think that the wizard surely thinks that the letter she wrote to you will convince you rather than anything I say."

The king says simply, "There is no doubt but what the letter is from the queen. I believe it was written recently, although I cannot be sure of that. She talks only of what she knows and remembers. She is sad at heart, but it is good, very good indeed, to know that she is alive."

The questions continue. "Has the wizard limited in any way what you can talk about?"

"No. In fact, he told me I can and should talk about anything you want. He realizes that only truth will get him what he wants, so he has started telling the truth. He instructed me to do the same."

Bollin pushes his chair back, has a brief word with his brother, and then with Cymbeline. He is aware that the wizard's ambassador should not sleep in the rooms of the Twith men. There may be secrets, such as Dayko's Rime, lying around loose. He feels the room he shares with his brother is probably the most suitable place for Vyruss to rest. Cymbeline agrees to help him make his bed and set the room straight. She has enough experience with Barney to not trust the tidying up abilities of boys. While they are bustling around out of sight, they check that the room is bare of anything that might possibly be useful to the wizard.

Cymbeline puts a glass of water on the table next to Bollin's immaculate bed. It is clad in clean sheets and pillowcase. Fresh pajamas are laid out on top. She hurries out to rejoin the others.

Vyruss is still answering questions. "What do you think happened to King Haymun?"

"I don't really know. I did hear someone moving around in the king's apartments at the castle. I think it must have been the king and not servants. Most likely, the wizard doesn't want him to know about Queen Sheba. He probably told him to keep out of the way."

"What is going to happen to you once the exchange is completed?"

"I'm not sure. The wizard may send me back to the border to complete the immigration control center."

"What happens if we decide against the proposal? Shouldn't you remain on the Brook with us?"

"No, I've given my word that I will go back to Gyminge and report whatever you decide. I will tell the wizard that I did my best." He closes his interview by smiling at them all. "I think it's better that you now consider your response without me. Do not hesitate to wake me if you need some further explanation." He pushes back his chair.

Bollin also rises. "I'll show you where you can rest."

Gerald has also pushed away from the table. "I have some salve for you to rub on your knuckles. It will relieve the soreness."

As they withdraw, Bimbo speaks to the king on behalf of the Shadow children. "What we heard from Vyruss will require careful consideration and great wisdom. Many things beyond the exchange itself are involved. It is the future of your kingdom that is involved. Perhaps we five Shadow children should give you space to talk freely among yourselves."

The king smiles and raises his hand. "No, please stay. I need your counsel, each of you. You two boys risked everything to bring back my sword and my shield from Gyminge. Shall I disregard you now? You girls have also proven yourselves. You will all undoubtedly go with us when we return to our own land. That will surely involve great risks. I insist you stay and be involved in the decision making."

He glances over at gran'ma. She is lost in thought. "Gumpa and gran'ma, we need to hear from you as well. I'm quite certain that gran'ma is wondering whether what happens today will affect her wedding plans. Feel free to share your thoughts, if you wish. Gerald, would you ask Ambro to join us? And, Cymbeline, would you go fetch my daughter?"

An extra chair is squeezed in next to the king's chair at the table. Bollin returns and confirms the ambassador is getting into bed. The bedroom door is closed. Some while elapses before the girls tiptoe in. Elisheba's eyes are glowing with added joy. She touches Taymar's shoulder as she passes on her way to embrace her father. Seating herself in the empty chair, she reaches out to hold her father's hand. "Oh, Daddy, can it really be true?"

The king responds with a smile and answers her only indirectly, addressing the whole crowded table. "I shall quickly summarize what we know and do not know. We will take time to discuss the questions lying before us. All of you should share your thoughts freely. I will then seek what response you would recommend to the proposal we just heard. The proposal is addressed to me and the response will be my own, but what each of you has to say will carry weight for my ultimate answer. Our Twith custom is to seek views consecutively from the most junior to the most senior so that all can speak freely in turn.

"The message brought by Dr. Tyfuss is from our longtime enemy, the Wizard of Wozzle. If we believe what the doctor told us, the message is genuine. However, the wizard's motives may not be. The message is clear. Exchange the genuine Twith Book of Lore for Queen Sheba who is in good health and able to come to the border. The letter Vyruss brought to me was unmistakably written in the queen's handwriting. It contains information that only the queen and I have knowledge of.

"Let me first ask Gerald. Do we in fact, at this time, possess the real and genuine Twith Book of Lore?"

"Yes, I can attest that we do."

"Then please take Taymar and Jordy with you and bring the Book of Lore from its hiding place. We will then verify whether the Lore contains within it a cure for the malady known as The Magician's Twitch. We are not in a position to meet the conditions of the proposal if that is not so."

The three Twith men go into Gerald's office and pull the door closed behind them. Immediately, there is some shuffling and shifting of chairs so that Taymar will sit on the other side of Elisheba when he returns. Cymbeline now sits next to Ambro. They hold hands beneath the table. The buzz of talking that broke out around the table goes quiet as they realize Cydlo is disclosing what was in his letter.

Elisheba tries to absorb all that her father says as he tells her the contents of her mother's letter. "Your mother is overjoyed to know that I am still alive. She feared I was dead because she had been told so. She has just been removed from the bottle the wizard put her in after she fell into his hands. Her bottle wasn't kept in the dungeons with the others, but in the hideaway room reached through the fireplace. You know the place. It's where I found you. She is uninjured and is being treated well. She heard that you had drowned in the lake and her heart is broken. She is pretty sure that the wizard has plans to use her to bargain with, but warned me not to trust him. She knows that the wizard cannot be trusted except to serve his own interests. She thinks the ambassador may be trustworthy, but she is unsure. She hopes to see me soon."

TABLE TALK

Gerald and the two others come back to the table from the office. Taymar closes the door behind them and smiles as he sees the place left empty beside Elisheba. He slides happily into it. Gerald places the Book of Lore on the table in front of him and looks towards Cydlo.

"Gerald, is this indeed the same Book of Lore that you brought from Gyminge when you fled?"

"Yes, this is the Book of Lore that has been with us since we left. It has been in my charge from that time to this. I know every mark within it."

"Does it have the cure for The Magician's Twitch in it?" It isn't really necessary for Cydlo to ask this. He, Gerald, Jock, and gran'ma all read it when she was typing the Lore into her computer to be saved. But he wants it verified in front of the others.

Gerald picks up the book from the table. He knows roughly where to look and quickly flicks through the leaves. He pulls his spectacles forward on his nose. He has a particular page open and is reading quickly. He turns the page.

"Here it is, right here. The title is underlined. _Cure for The Magician's Twitch_."

"Gerald, will you read it through quickly to yourself and tell me, does it actually prescribe the cure for The Magician's Twitch?"

"Yes, that's exactly what it does. It doesn't discuss much about the ailment itself, but it explains the remedy. I am sure this is what the wizard wants. If he gets this, he will be quite content."

"Very well. Remain with us, Gerald. You can put the Book of Lore back later." The king continues, "The wizard is telling us that he wants the Book of Lore because he needs the cure for The Magician's Twitch. That might very well not be the whole story.

Perhaps just as significant to him will be the Lore itself, and that may be what he really wants. This holds all the wisdom of our people. It sets the standards and principles we live by. It contains all the counsel by which we live together in harmony and cooperation. It tells how good people can resist and overcome the plans and tricks of evil men and how they can detect deceit and counter it. All we know about healing, about justice and punishment and mercy, about rulers and the ruled, about loyalty and love of country and others, about weapons and tactics, about nature and medicines and poisons and remedies is all in the Lore. All we know about the enemies that beset us and their weaknesses is there as well.

"Gerald, you know better than any man what the Lore contains. Can we even consider tying our hands behind our backs to let our worst and most determined enemy possess all our wisdom?"

"How can I answer, Sire? The protection of the Book of Lore has been my concern above everything else other than our survival to carry on until we return. The wizard has already defeated us once. His magic already gives him immense power. To give him the Book of Lore will surely double the power he already has. When he is able to combine that with the power that truth and wisdom have brought a whole people, who will be able to withstand him then? Gyminge and Wozzle will be too small for him. I'm sure he intends to conquer the world. I would still be prepared to do so if that were the choice before me. Yet that is not the choice. We have a different choice and the wizard has laid it before us. Dayko foresaw the choice we would be facing today. His counsel does not lie in the Lore but in the Rime."

> *The loss of the Lore gives grief*
> *Though what is that to a life?*

"Surely, Dayko foresaw the quandary we face today when he wrote this. The life that is balanced against the Book of Lore is that of our queen. When we discussed this not long ago, none of us dreamed that this would, could, be the choice placed before us. We saw it in other terms then. We thought Dayko was trying to guide us by suggesting a life, even the humblest life, is certainly worth more than a book written by men long dead. I have been prepared to give my life to protect the Lore. But now, it is the queen's life we are talking about. It doesn't matter how valuable the book might be. Dayko did not give us the answer to whether we should give up the Book of Lore—that remains our decision—but he is reminding us where the division really lies. The wizard has made no suggestion as to what he might do to the queen if we should not agree to his proposal. He, very wisely from his viewpoint, chose to leave that to our imaginations."

The king turns to gran'ma. "Gran'ma, you have made some kind of copy of the Lore on your machine upstairs. Can you be sure that your machine will not lose it? If it does and the Book of Lore is exchanged, we will be left with nothing."

Gran'ma is confident about her procedure for saving the Lore. "I have a copy of the Lore on disc that can be read into any computer if mine should happen to fail. I also put a copy of the Lore on Gumpa's computer. At present, we have three copies of it available."

However, she too is suddenly uneasy. "Cydlo, as soon as this meeting is over, I will go upstairs and print out a copy of the Lore and give it to Gerald. I am satisfied that what we have upstairs is safe, but before you send Dr. Tyfuss off with our reply, I want to be sure that we are not putting ourselves at any risk of being without a true copy of the Lore."

Cydlo nods his satisfaction and suggests another consideration before he seeks individual opinions.

"We have considered the Book of Lore. Now let us think about the queen. She has told me in her letter that she has been kept bottled in captivity for centuries and she thinks that the wizard has removed her to use her to bargain with. The queen counsels, 'Do not trust him. He cannot be trusted except to serve his own interests.'

"Let me ask you. Do you think that we can trust the wizard? In other words, are we offered a straightforward bargain where both parties deal and act straight or is this all part of a vast trickery to outwit us and gain the upper hand over us? If we trust him in this instance, what next? If we do not, what next? What do you think he will do to the queen if we refuse his proposal? Can I have one or two of your thoughts about that?"

Gran'ma raises her hand.

Cydlo nods towards her. "Yes, gran'ma, what are your thoughts?"

She is unsure of herself and speaks softly, "You ask whether the wizard can be trusted. The queen brings her knowledge of the past to bear when she says do not trust him. We know that his nature and character are definitely untrustworthy so her counsel is wise. However, she is unaware of the series of defeats that the wizard has recently suffered. He has not been doing well at all. He was repulsed here on the Brook and also in Gyminge. I was released from captivity, you and the princess brought here, and the sword and the shield recovered from the very castle he lives in. Those are some major defeats for the wizard.

"He is desperate for a victory. This proposal offers it. And what will it cost him? Nothing except the contents of a stored bottle that has been gathering dust in storage for hundreds of years. The queen has value to him in only one way, as a hostage. To turn her into a bargaining pawn means that he will gain everything for nothing. He tried it before with me, but only succeeded in splitting your forces in two. The fact that he failed to take advantage of that was due to your bravery.

"Why should he try to keep the queen by trickery? What good would that do him? Vyruss told us that in this matter, he believes the wizard can be trusted. I think so too. He is using the last weapon he has available—truth.

"You ask what might happen to the queen if you reject his proposal. At this point, he probably hasn't even considered you will do so. He will surely keep her as a hostage for later use when he may be in difficulty. She is insurance for the wizard and he will not harm her. Only if she has no further possible value for him is he likely to do so."

THE BEYONDERS' RESPONSE

Cydlo puts up his hand to indicate a halt. "We have all the time we need to talk, but will further discussion actually resolve things? I think the issues before us are clear enough and we should move on. I will now ask each of you, our Beyonder friends first, to express your opinion on the response that I should make. Let your answer be clearly either 'Yes', meaning you feel we should accept the wizard's proposal or 'No', meaning that we should not. If you wish to add a brief explanation of your answer, please do so."

Cydlo look over at the Shadow children. "Girls, the three of you are sitting together. What do each of you feel?"

Margaret answers first, "I think the wizard will only have a short while to take advantage of whatever is in the Book of Lore. The quicker we move against him, the better. I vote yes."

Ruthie is next. "Yes, we can survive the loss of the Lore. We don't know what will happen to the queen if we refuse. We mustn't risk her now that we have the opportunity to save her."

Ellie answers simply, "Yes, give up the Lore. It would be wrong to not save the life of the queen when we have the chance to do so."

The king looks across at Bimbo. The boy is puzzled. "We don't know how, but the wizard already found a way to discover what goes on in Twith Mansion. This isn't an easy decision, and I'm just not sure. We're playing right into the wizard's hands if we give him the Lore. I think it is the whole Lore the wizard wants and not just the cure for his twitchy eye. That's an immediate benefit, but that's just part of it. Beyond that lies much more. When he gets his hands on the Book of Lore, he will read it from cover to cover within twenty-four hours. Whatever he didn't know about the Twith before will become a weapon he can and certainly will use against us. We will be fighting a much stronger enemy, and he will be much more difficult to defeat. We will have to stay alert and be very careful. He will see a yes answer from us as a stepping-stone on the way to victory over us and our complete defeat. However, although I have much anxiety, I agree with the others. My answer, too, is yes."

Bollin, sitting next to Bimbo, follows without being asked. "Yes. Although it will be much harder to fight the wizard when his eye doesn't twitch, we must take that chance. A life is a life and that has to come first."

The king turns to Gumpa and gran'ma. He has only known them a little over two weeks, but this is more than enough time for him to love and appreciate them.

Gran'ma is anxious to give her opinion and then disengage herself and get upstairs to her computer. She has responsibilities for a double wedding less than three days away. She also has sixteen houseguests, and although they show remarkable resilience and energy and undoubted abilities, an older voice of guidance is helpful to guide their enthusiasm down the right track. "The proposal sounds straightforward. And if it truly is a straightforward swap, then I would have to say yes. But it goes far beyond that. The wizard gets and absorbs all the wisdom of the Twith. A battle to the end with the wizard lies ahead, and the odds were heavily against us even before this. The struggle promises to be in the wizard's own territory behind a barrier that prevents the help of the birds. It is a task that now becomes almost impossible. However, I still say yes. When all is said and done, the future is what we choose to make it, no matter how dark the clouds are. I will stay to hear what Gumpa has to say, but then, may I please be excused to see to things upstairs?"

Attention now turns to her husband. He is uneasy, and his brow is creased. Gumpa tends to be long-winded, but he realizes that in order to work this through for a possible teatime exchange, Vyruss has to be awakened soon and sent on his way. "Every instinct I have says no. To deal with the wizard on his terms means we are being brought down to his level. When we deal with a deceiver, we must expect to be deceived. We know that even the slightest slip from complete truthfulness can deny us the Return indefinitely, possibly even forever. By dealing with him on his terms, how can we know that he won't trap us into a lie in order to save the queen? He could easily make a trap that requires the mere twisting of only a few words away from the truth.

"He may have calculated, Cydlo, that your love for the queen is likely to be stronger than your love for the truth. There will be no question in his mind how you will answer. He will try to exploit that when he has you before him, offering your queen in exchange for a few insignificant words. And if we try to outwit this man of tricks and lies, we ourselves will take part in a lie that goes against our agreement to avoid trickery.

"There was a verse I learned in my childhood. It was called *Disintegration*. I remember it well for I found it to be powerfully true.

> *Strange—*
> *That the lie*
> *That cost me*
> *My courage*
> *And my character*
> *And innocence*
> *And integrity*
> *And the trust of those*
> *Who live around me*

*Was so powerful—
and so insignificant.*

"I am full of fear for you, Cydlo, and for all of us here. Yet in spite of my fear, my answer is also yes."

THE RESPONSE OF
THE TWITH

The king sighs as he hears what Gumpa has to say. It reaffirms his own thinking. The Beyonders have all given their replies, and gran'ma quietly slips her chair away from the table. As she does so, Margaret and Ellie do so as well. The girls know that the children upstairs will be full of curiosity. Someone needs to fill them in on what's been happening. They put their three chairs back in the kitchen to make more space around the table.

Jordy knows gran'ma will need help from a Twith to become Beyonder-size again. He whispers to Cydlo, "I'll be back in a moment." He follows her up the passage towards the staircase to upstairs.

Cydlo does not wait for Jordy to return. He starts with the youngest Twith. "Barney, will you share with us what you think? Should we accept the wizard's proposal?"

Barney thinks as a boy thinks. Straight from the question to the answer. For him, there are no complications. "I wouldn't know what to think if it wasn't for Dayko. He didn't give us the answer, but he told us what the question really is. I think he also suggested the answer we should give. My answer is yes."

Cymbeline is next. She has a gentle heart and she loves Elisheba as a dear sister. "You know that Elisheba is getting married on Friday. She needs for her mother to be at her wedding. And if her mother knew about the wedding, she would want to be there. It will be too late if we wait to work out her release at some later date. It has to be right soon and the wizard is making it possible! My answer is yes." She thinks, *What clothes do I have upstairs that the queen could possibly wear? Will she be the same size as Elisheba?*

Jordy slips back quietly into his seat.

Ambro knows he is the next oldest and doesn't wait for Cydlo to call on him. "I was in a bottle possibly as long as the queen. Everyone in a bottle wants to escape, and eventually, I managed to get free. The wizard is demanding almost the highest price that he can for the freedom of the queen—the wisdom of the Twith through the ages. If we say no, the queen will likely be returned to the captivity of her bottle with all its despair and hopelessness. The wizard is probably unlikely to do worse to her than that, but it will break her heart. To yield the Book of Lore will certainly make our return to Gyminge more difficult, perhaps as gran'ma says, nearly impossible. But is anything ever really impossible while courage holds? My answer is yes."

Although it is Elisheba's turn next, Cydlo stops her. "I'd like for you to go last, my sweet." She smiles and nods her head.

Taymar is madly in love. He holds Elisheba's hand tightly and she squeezes back. He and Ambro are the sons of Earl Gareth of Up-Horton. "Our father trained us boys to say and do what is right irrespective of the consequences. Our parents built within us a framework of good judgment and high principles. That enables me to discover for myself what is right. There are often two courses of apparent equal merit. Making difficult decisions that are right is part of wise leadership. A man should listen to others, but decide for himself and then act. To deal with a man as treacherous as the wizard repels me. In this case, although it promises additional difficulties and many dangers, it will be right to accept the wizard's offer. My answer is yes."

Jordy has been listening carefully. "So far all have answered yes although with deep concerns and strong reservations. The question is the future of Gyminge. That is not the land of my birth, I am from the north, but I fought for its freedom and I will do so again. Through the long centuries of the Exile, I adopted the distant dream of a possible return to Gyminge into my own heart. And I'm thinking that I probably will not go back north when it is all over. I'll stay with the rest of you. There'll be much work to do in putting Gyminge back on its feet. The question for me is whether a yes or a no answer will bring us closer to a permanent return home. I agree that there will be some consequences of the wizard absorbing and using all the wisdom in the Lore. The odds against us, however, should never bother us. Victory often falls to the few in number." Suddenly, surprising even to himself, Jordy finds himself thirsting for a fight. "If that's the way the wizard wants it, then let him have it. My answer is yes."

There are just three men left to reply. Cydlo turns to Gerald. "Before you give us your opinion, I'd be interested to know your thoughts about whether the cure for the Twitch is likely to be immediate or gradual. If it is immediate, it will make no difference. But if it is gradual, the quicker we move against him the better."

Gerald responds, "I would think that just as the twitch itself grows gradually, so the remedy will take place gradually. When a sick person takes his medicine regularly, he is likely to recover more quickly than one who does not. We can be sure that the wizard will not be slack in his effort to be completely cured. He will cause it to work as fast as he can."

Within the last week, the king appointed Gerald to be the High Seer of Gyminge. His responsibility is to maintain and protect the Twith Book of Lore. He is ready to die to protect it. During all the centuries of exile, the Twith have relied on Gerald to take care of the Book of Lore and have been relaxed that it is in the safest possible hands. He recently spent many hours, including hours when he might have been sleeping, creating a pseudo Book of Lore. That was what the wizard stole. And now, the wizard is attempting to obtain the actual book by straightforward negotiation. "You give me the Book of Lore and I'll give you your queen."

Gerald wonders, *Can I, as the High Seer, be true to my office if I agree to give the Book of Lore to the wizard?*

He heaves a great sigh. "I believe that our highest ideals call upon us to not only sacrifice ourselves but, even more difficult, to sacrifice those dearest to us for the common good. And that involves judgments we must each make. I believe we should accept the wizard's proposal, so I answer yes. We must do it with complete honesty and truth. Whether the wizard does wrong or not, we must not play any tricks. If we accept the offer made to us, we accept his conditions and do not try to circumvent them. We must not try to outwit him because we must be true to ourselves."

Jock has been unusually silent throughout this morning. Ever since Vyruss arrived on the doorstep, the Scot has been quietly guiding events when necessary, but he has been content to be silent when Cydlo came forward to take his place as king. He listens with great care and complete interest to every speaker. Some of the answers clearly surprise him. He was expecting the responses to be much more mixed.

"As ye all know, I 'ave 'ad vast experience with th' wizard's trickery 'n' deceit 'n' ruthlessness. I've encountered 'is determination o'er th' centuries in places all o'er th' world. Th' man will simply stop a' nuthin ta git wha' 'e wants. Ta turn o'er th' Book o' Lore is like a soldier turnin' o'er all 'is weapons ta 'is enemy who is armed ta th' teeth, 'n' then sayin', 'Le' battle commence'. I 'ave mixed feelin's, bu' thur seems ta be nay alternative." He answers slowly and with resignation. "I will say yes. Bu' I agree with Gerald. We mus' be true ta ourselves. We cun nay counter th' wizard's tricks with our own. We mus' open our 'ands 'n' le' 'im see tha' they are empty 'n' accept th' consequences."

Stumpy has always loved his king and queen. The continuing leadership of his country rests in a family whose love is their duty, to serve the people and be servants to them. He was delighted to discover that the woodsman and his daughter are his king and his princess. His response is short. "The Book of Lore is important, but we must free the queen while we can. The king needs and deserves his wife. Tomorrow the choice may not be there. I quite often differ from the rest of you in my opinions, but this time I agree. My answer is yes."

There is only one answer left to seek. Cydlo turns to his daughter.

Elisheba has had her whole world transformed for her this morning. She has not seen her mother since her parents sent her into hiding to a cottage in Blindhouse Wood more than a thousand years ago. At that time, the invasion from Wozzle was only a subject for discussion across the castle meal table. It was not yet a reality.

All of a sudden, her mother is less than a few hours away. She was told by the wizard that her only child is long dead. Elisheba's heart cries out, *No, Mummy, that's not true, I'm alive, I'm here and I'm well and I'm about to be married and I want you to be here! I need you, Mummy!*

She is delighted that everyone around the table has affirmed that her father should accept the wizard's offer. She was sure that some would advise against the proposal, but no one has. She needs no more time to think through her answer. She tosses it out to her father with dancing eyes and a radiant face. "Yes, Daddy. Yes! Please!"

Cydlo sighs. "Thank you all. Listening to you has been a great help and it has served to change my mind. Elisheba and Ambro, will you please leave us for a while? It will probably still be best that the ambassador does not know you are here. Gran'ma will need help if she wants to come back down again. Please be ready to assist her.

"Bollin, would you be good enough to go wake Vyruss? The rest of you may get up and stretch until the doctor comes in. I need to do that myself. Cymbeline, it is getting close to lunch-time. Could you arrange some nourishment for us?"

The girl scurries off to the kitchen, followed closely by Gumpa and Ruthie.

THE ANSWER

Jordy sorts out the correct number of chairs that will now be needed around the table. Jock pulls Barney aside. "Crusty needs ta stay on duty a' th' farm'ouse, so will ye go ask Maggie or one o' th' other birds ta go fetch Tuwhi' fur me? Ask the same bird ta then go tell Buffo ta wai' a' th' croc' pond ta take th' ambassador ta th' waterfall. Thanks." The boy scurries off.

While they wait, Cydlo, Jock, and Gerald talk quietly among themselves. Gerald has not yet put the Book of Lore away. His hand rests lightly on top of it, his fingers stroking the cover as though saying good-bye to a good friend. He is thinking again about Dayko's Rime and its reference to the flag. *Black and white the flag high will rise, The Child shall lead on to the Prize.* He rewords it in his mind. *The black-and-white flag will rise high (in victory for the wizard) and then the Child shall lead on to the Prize.* It triggers thoughts again about the Child. *We know that—because the word 'child' is capitalized—it is one of the Beyonder children who have come to help us. But which one?*

Bollin and Bimbo have been in their bedroom chatting with Vyruss as he gets ready. All three come out together. Although he is their friend, the two boys have been guarded in giving Vyruss any new information that the wizard could later wheedle out of him.

Cymbeline and Ruthie prepare vegetables for stew. The water in the great saucepan is simmering. Gumpa is busy mixing up dough for dumplings and has succeeded in getting flour all over himself. This is in spite of the wrap-around apron Cymbeline swaddled him in.

Margaret, Ellie, and gran'ma come down from upstairs. Gran'ma chuckles with amusement when she sees the mess her husband has made. She turns and gives the thumbs-up sign to Gerald. "I've printed off the Lore from the computer. All that remains is to bind it and shrink it down to the correct size."

All other activity is set to one side as Vyruss comes in and bows towards Cydlo and settles back into a chair. Cymbeline moves her saucepan off the heat. The three-kitchen crew join the others around the table.

The king asks Vyruss, "Did you manage to get any sleep?"

"Yes, thank you. I slept like a log."

"All right then. Let's resume our discussion. Mr. Ambassador, I want you to report to the wizard that I accept his proposal on the terms and conditions he has laid out. I shall comply with them in their entirety. The time I suggest for the exchange is five o'clock this afternoon. The place where the exchange will be made will be the location at the curtain where the goblin forces on the Brook withdrew back to Gyminge. I understand the wizard also used that same place to leave the Brook with Rasputin last Thursday. This will be a place known to them although not yet known to me. We shall mark it on our side with the black-and-white flag that you brought with you. That will probably be visible through the curtain.

"I confirm to you also that the Book of Lore has been examined. It has been on the Brook and in the care of Gerald since it was brought from Gyminge. You may wish to question him about it."

"Yes, that would be helpful." Vyruss proceeds to do so. "Gerald, is that the Book of Lore on the table before you?"

"Yes, it is. This is the book that I brought with me when I left Gyminge and I have been responsible for the care of it ever since."

"Is it complete in every way? Have any pages, or parts of pages, or any of its contents been removed from it?"

"No, nothing has been removed from it. It is complete."

"Have any alterations or insertions been made to it?"

"No. The only one who can authorize additions to the Book of Lore is the High Seer of Gyminge. Dayko's death meant there was no one to authorize any alterations or additions and none have been made."

"Does the Lore contain a remedy for The Magician's Twitch?"

"Yes, it does. I have placed a bookmark in the place where it occurs."

"I do not need to see or read the remedy itself, but will you please bring the Book of Lore around so that I may see the title of the section for myself?"

Gerald realizes that Vyruss is not questioning his word but fulfilling his own instructions from the one who has sent him. He eases his chair back and takes the book around to the ambassador.

"May I hold and examine the closed book first?"

Gerald hands it to Vyruss, and he looks carefully at the binding, the inscriptions on the cover, and the edges of the pages. He opens to where the bookmark is and reads the title: *Cure for The Magician's Twitch*. He closes the book without reading further.

"Thank you, Gerald. Will you give me your word that until the exchange is made, there will be no attempt in any way to change the content of the Lore from what it is now? I will reexamine the Lore just prior to the exchange."

"Yes, I give you my word."

"Jock, will you give me your word that as far as you know, this is the full and complete Lore, that it has in no way been altered nor is it in any way deficient of any of its contents? Also that there will be no attempt to change the content of the Lore before the time of its exchange for the queen."

"Aye, I give ye me word."

Vyruss turns at last back to the king. "Sire, I mean no disrespect. Can I ask you for your word also that as far as you know this is the full and complete Lore, that it has in no way been altered nor is it in any way deficient of any of its contents? Also that there will be no attempt to change the content of the Lore before the time of its exchange for the queen."

Cydlo smiles. This is all part of the bargain. "Yes, I give you my word."

Vyruss pushes back his chair. He stands at attention. He bows towards the king and then to both sides of the table and all those seated there.

"I thank you for your courtesy to me. If you would kindly arrange for me to see the location of the exchange, I will mark it with the flag as you suggested. With your help, I will then head for the waterfall and cause your message to reach the wizard as soon as possible. I am sure that the time you suggest will give adequate time for the travelers on the other side to meet as agreed."

Cymbeline speaks up. "Lunch is nearly ready, Vyruss. Please stay and have something to eat before you leave."

The ambassador shakes his head. "No, thank you just the same. I'm sorry, but I'm anxious to be on my way." He really is sorry. He would like nothing better than to bask in Cymbeline's beauty over a meal table.

Jock, Jordy, Gerald, and Cydlo accompany him outside. Jock whistles for Tuwhit. All five climb on Tuwhit's back. He knows exactly where the wizard and his troops disappeared under the curtain. Last Thursday while the circus was setting up, he followed the wizard and Rasputin as they left the Brook. The wizard walked on the surface above the new mole tunnel until he encountered the curtain. There, he pulled up the bottom of the curtain to allow himself and the raven under and through into Gyminge.

Tuwhit carries the black-and-white flag in his beak. It is safer there than if Vyruss were carrying it. Few flags fly as high as this one.

The owl sees where the line of molehills ends and recognizes the small hole where the mole with the bent nose had discharged. Behind him, Sergeant Aga had tried to imitate a propeller driven aerial torpedo in pursuit of the runaway mole. He was almost immediately smothered by over eight hundred goblin soldiers. Last of all came King Haymun who landed on top of the heap. There is no sign of any activity now. Tuwhit lands close by. This is where they will plant the flag to mark where the exchange of the Book of Lore and the queen will take place.

In the nearby mole tunnel, Jacko has yet to emerge into the daylight, although he is close enough to see light at the end of the tunnel. His sides are raw with scraping through a tunnel too small for him. There is nothing more lonely than a ferret stuck in a single use mole tunnel a quarter of a mile long. He has been more lonely than Robinson Crusoe on his island! Because it is a single use tunnel designed for escape to Gyminge, there were no friendly moles to help him. It was highly unlikely that one would come scurrying along and say, "Hi, fella! Having a spot of bother? Let me give you a paw."

It is unfortunate for Jacko that he isn't a mole. Moles are professional tunnel diggers. A mole's front and back paws are designed for the job. It's fur is thick around his eyes and the dirt sticks to it, so he digs with his eyes closed to prevent dirt getting into them. He uses his nose to help. Because its ears are merely holes in his head covered with fur, they don't stick out and get jammed up against the sides of the tunnel. A mole can go backwards and forwards in his tunnel, although he normally likes to dig in a forward direction. His fat little roly-poly body pushes the loose dirt into the sides of the tunnel as he wriggles his way forward following his nose. A mole is perfectly designed for digging tunnels.

Jacko finally makes it to the exit. It has probably helped, although he didn't think so at the time, that he missed out on a meal last night. He is just about to push his exhausted nose gratefully out into the open air when he hears noises. Quickly, he pulls his head back in out of sight. Noises, especially owl noises and Twith voices, spell danger for a secret agent. In the darkness, he shakes the dirt out of his ears and bangs his head in the process. The first voice he hears is Jock's.

"This is th' spot, Vyruss. Plant th' flag deep in th' molehill dirt so i' won't fall o'er. Push i' in 'ard. This is where we will put th' Book o' Lore. Gerald, will ye please pace back forty paces where Vyruss 'n' Cydlo will need ta stand? Jordy, will ye go back a further sixty paces 'n' mark th' boundary where th' res' o' us mus' be?

"Are ye satisfied with this arrangemen', Vyruss? When ye are, Tuwhi' will drop ye off a' th' edge o' th' bog. After 'e takes us 'ome, 'e will cum back 'n' wait in th' tree 'til ye return. Buffo is waitin' ta hop ye o'er ta th' waterfall. 'E will stay thur 'n' wai' ta bring ye back 'cross th' bog. Then Tuwhi' will bring ye back ta th' mansion 'til i' is time ta cum back this afternoon ta make th' exchange. We will 'ave th' Book o' Lore ready fur ye ta verify as th' wizard asked. I'll 'ave Cymbeline prepare a meal fur when ye git back. I know thur is much other news fur ye ta share 'n' we look forward ta wha' ye 'ave ta say. Ye 'ave th' time clear? Five o'clock this afternoon."

There is a murmur of voices, a sound of farewells, wings beat the air, and then there is silence.

THE COTTAGE

Jacko waits for some time before he slowly pokes his nose and then his head out of the mole tunnel. A black flag with a large white circle on it flies from a pole stuck in the molehill. All else is silence. No sign of any life. "Hmm! Very interesting. Five o'clock they said. Well, I'm going to make a point of being back here before five o'clock."

Before he departs, he checks for nearby hiding places where he will be well hidden. "I expect that the mole tunnel and also rabbit burrows will be too obvious as hiding places, although either might prove a useful way of escape." He checks quickly where the nearest burrows are, but none are close enough to suit him.

He chooses for his hideaway a deep thicket of bracken and bramble and stinging nettles towards Cope farm. "This will do very nicely. It is only about half as far from the flag as the forty pace pebble marker that Gerald placed. I'll clear a space while no one is around." He clears away all scrub down to the dirt itself, but leaves plenty of foliage for cover. To avoid being seen when he returns, he will once more use the mole tunnels from Mole Hall all the way to the flag. Now that he has successfully made it through once, there should be no difficulty in getting through again.

Satisfied with his preparations, he heads for home. "I need to do some social calling, but I will have to be back and in place at least an hour early to be sure I don't miss out on anything."

The ferret ponders his choices for a meal. "Mrs. Squidge's cooking does leave something to be desired from a meat-eater's point of view. However, when you are hungry, it doesn't pay to be too fussy." He reminds himself, "I mustn't eat much at Squidgy's lest my girth later cause me trouble in the tunnel. I also need to get more information about what I just overheard. The SnuggleWump rarely knows anything useful, but Cajjer and his mistress must surely know what is going on."

He runs quickly on the surface through the bracken, which forms a canopy above him. When he is out in the open, he has to be alert for possible air patrols. He considers every bird on the Brook a possible enemy. "They all favor the rabbits and are the first to give warning when they spot me." He also runs in a wide, twisting course to spread his scent. "That should help keep the rabbits out of the way this afternoon on the north end of the Brook!" He runs up close to the farmhouse path and then backtracks towards Brook Lane until he is eventually near enough to cut for home.

He wastes no time going to Mole Hall; his pantry is empty. He greets the SnuggleWump as he passes, ignores as usual the teros on the ridge of the cottage, and runs up the steps to the front porch. He knocks on the door with a confident *Ra-ta-tat-tat*. It is answered by a groan from inside. He knocks again, a little less noisily, and again, a groan answers him.

He stands on his hind legs, turns the doorknob, and pushes the door partway open. He looks in and sighs. "It doesn't look as though afternoon tea is likely to be any time soon."

Mrs. Squidge sits in her rocking chair at the fireplace. Both of her legs are up on the other chair. She removed her boots and they are lying where she took them off. On her chin is a very large Band-Aid. Around her forehead is a damp tea towel knotted at the back. There is a bloodied bandage around her right hand and wrist and more large Band-Aids on the back of her left hand and higher up on her wrist.

Beside her lies an almost unrecognizable Cajjer. It is his licorice swirl stripes and the shortened length of his tail that identify him, not his appearance. His head appears to have doubled in size. His eyes are only pinholes in what appears to be either one continuous bruise or the partially successful first oversize transplant of a turnip with ears onto the body of a cat. Balanced on his head is a dishtowel containing cold parsnips. Occasionally, the cat dips it into a bowl of water to cool it down. Cajjer meows weakly in a continuous, shrill, distressed squeak like a stuck police siren.

Jacko thinks, *I'm not much of a gentleman. Such instincts don't even come close. However, Mrs. Squidge and Cajjer are near neighbors. I suppose I should find out what's wrong. I may even have to be generous and offer to help.* He steps inside and pushes the door closed. He coughs. "Are you having trouble, Mrs. Squidge? Hello, Cajjer, how are you doing?"

He gets only groans in reply.

He tries again. "Is there something I can do to help? You look as though you could do with a cup of tea. Shall I put the kettle on?"

More groans issue forth. Mrs. Squidge doesn't stir and neither does Cajjer.

If I wait much longer, it will be my tummy that's groaning!

The Cornish range in the back kitchen that the lady of the house uses for her cooking has not been lit. This is no difficulty for a ferret who sparkles with ingenuity and intelligence. The kindling is there and the local newspaper. He jumps onto the cold stove and pulls back the iron plate that covers the burned-out fire. He scratches around inside with his paw to drop the ashes through to the ashtray. Tearing up some newspaper, he drops that in and adds a bit of kindling. He then lifts up several lumps of coal onto the flat surface of the range ready to push in. The first match he lights flickers out before catching the paper on fire. The second match ignites the paper. As the kindling begins to blaze, Jacko gives the coal lumps a sweep with his paw and pushes the round lid back into place. A pot of water is already sitting on the range and he shoves it over onto the fire lid. Quickly, he jumps onto the floor before his paws get too hot.

The kindling crackles and sparks. There is a roar as the hot air pushes up the chimney. Jacko partly closes the damper. He sees that the pantry door is open, so while the water is getting hot, he does some exploring. "I remember Squidgy's vicious swipe at the wizard when he dared to take a bite out of one of her yeast buns! No way am I going to touch any of those! I doubt she will notice if a couple of her sausages are missing." He hungrily wolfs down one and then takes another. He could easily consume two more, but he remembers, "I need to be careful how much I eat. I don't want to get stuck in that tunnel again." Feeling better, he checks the fire and then returns to check on his hostess and her cat.

His rather rasping voice sounds like a file being scraped backwards over the edge of a piece of tin can. "Mrs. Squidge, if you can tell me where you keep your tea, I'll make you a pot. It will make you feel better."

Squidgy recognizes that the ferret is just trying to be helpful, but she shudders inwardly. *It won't make me feel better if the ferret makes it! What ferrets don't know about making tea would fill a book.* The woman groans again and rises painfully to her feet. It is not just the bandaged parts of her body that hurt. She hurts all over. "No, Mr. Jacko, you just sit down and talk to Cajjer and try to cheer him up. He's in a worse way than I am. I'm feeling somewhat better now."

So is the ferret. *It's amazing what a pair of sausages will do for your outlook on life when you are hungry.*

Griselda doesn't want him sitting in her chair. Forgetting to stop groaning, she pulls a stool over close to Cajjer for the ferret and goes slowly out to the kitchen. Moving around seems to help and the soreness of her bruised body eases a bit. She forgets she is not wearing shoes and gives the twig broom a kick as she passes. It makes her wince. "Ouch! That hurts."

It isn't long before Squidgy carries a tray back into the living room. She didn't use her precious Darjeeling tea this time. *English breakfast tea is good enough for the ferret.*

Jacko sips his tea slowly and nibbles at his biscuit. He begins the conversation carefully. He learned long ago that knowledge is money and silence is golden when you are trying to earn a living. "I gather you have had a fall, Mrs. Squidge?"

"A fall! That's only part of it. All because I was trying to do the wizard a good turn."

Jacko holds back a smile. *This is the opening I've been looking for.* "Oh, the wizard. Have you heard from him since the circus?"

"Yes, this morning after we got back from being out. Rasputin came with a letter, but he had to leave again right away. I was just as glad. Since I'm not feeling all that well, I fear I wasn't as welcoming as I should have been. The wizard appreciated our help during his recent visit and may come again soon. He is most hopeful that he will soon be in possession of the Twith Book of Lore. You know how keen he is to obtain that. I sometimes think he would give half of all he possesses just for that one book. It is amazing the fascination some books have for real scholars like the wizard. For myself, I prefer magazines or an occasional cookbook."

The ferret leans forward. This is exactly the kind of news he wanted to hear. He holds back his excitement as he asks casually, "Did he say anything more about his plans?"

"Not a thing. He just said things seem to be going well." She goes on to tell him about her day as far as she understands it. She is somehow glad to have someone to talk it over with even though it is only the ferret. She is trying to understand all that actually happened and telling about it seems to help clear up some of the confusion. Cajjer isn't ready for bright and sparkling conversation.

The ferret isn't really listening. He is watching the clock and working on thoughts and plans of his own.

THE RENDEZVOUS

It is a fine afternoon with a few cirrus clouds high and distant in a deep blue sky. The warm sun is softened by a light breeze. At about a quarter to five, Crusty leaves to take a full load of observers down to the curtain. Tuwhit will shortly be taking Dr. Tyfuss, Gerald, and Cydlo. The only ones staying behind to take care of things at the farmhouse are Gumpa and gran'ma. The sparrow hawk and the kestrel are on the roof keeping their eyes open. Cymbeline and Ambro will stay behind to guard Twith Mansion.

Before leaving, Gerald and Cydlo are chatting with Dr. Tyfuss about the future in Gyminge. Vyruss shares what he learned from observing the group habits of woodlouses. "People would benefit from ordering their societies in the same way as woodlouses. One for all and all for one!"

The Book of Lore is on the dining table. Vyruss, as the Ambassador of Gyminge to the Beyond, has satisfied himself that it is the same book as the one he examined this morning. A plastic shopping bag and some string for tying it into a secure bundle are beside it.

The doctor will miss these Twith he has become acquainted with on the Brook. More and more, he begins to feel like one of them himself. It has come as a deep shock to him to hear that Cymbeline is about to marry another of the Twith. He had to draw on all his reserves of inner strength to avoid betraying emotion. Strange thoughts flit through his mind. *I wonder whether she has a sister? This is not the time to ask that question, though.*

As Cymbeline bustles about cleaning up after the meal she prepared for him, he tells her, "Although I have not met the bridegroom-to-be, he is a very, very fortunate man to marry such a lovely bride."

Cymbeline flushes and turns back to her dishes at the sink. "You are most welcome to attend the wedding. It will be this coming Friday here at the farm."

"Well, I don't know what plans the wizard will now have for me. I will certainly be happy to come and join the wedding party if it proves possible."

Jock has gone ahead with the others to make sure that the wizard's instructions are carefully followed. Crusty lands where directed by Jordy, at the stone marker a hundred paces distant from the curtain. The eagle will take a position in his nest high in the oak tree when the transaction actually takes place. Jock paces back a further twenty paces. He doesn't want any snags because the wizard thinks the observers are too near. Specs and Bajjer form two distant ends of an imaginary line. Everyone must stand behind this line. The best vantage point, a molehill making a rise in the ground, is given to Elisheba and Taymar. Stumpy rests his hand on Barney's shoulder for support. Specs checks his watch. Only a few minutes left.

A dozen or so paces further back, wherever the bracken is not so thick and dense, badgers are watching what is happening. Blackie and the other rabbits are hiding deep in their burrows. Blackie watches from the mouth of one of the burrows ready to either retreat back in or dart into the bracken. The word has gone out that the ferret is hunting. For more than a week, none of their own company has been lost. Jacko is probably starving.

Micah, using Gumpa's binoculars that work, spots a titchy raven with a broken beak in the distant field over in Gyminge. Rasputin perches in an ash tree, the highest in the hedge. There is no sign of the wizard yet or, more important to some, the lady he will bring with him.

As Tuwhit flies in, there is a stir of excitement. He knows where to land without being told. He sets down beside Gerald's stone that marks forty paces. Lowering himself to the ground, his three passengers dismount.

Cydlo is not yet nimble. Under Elisheba's final check and guidance, he has dressed carefully and is wearing his best clothes, those he plans to wear at the wedding. He has a white rose bud in his buttonhole and is carrying a bouquet of Gumpa's best pink rosebuds. Stormy picked and arranged them and then shrunk them with Barney's help.

Gerald carries the Book of Lore in the bag. The string to tie it is in his pocket.

Dr. Tyfuss left his overcoat back in Gyminge and feels more comfortable.

The mallard, finally brave enough to return home, found the ambassador's hat floating among the weeds. He inquired at the farmhouse whether this might perhaps belong to his recent passenger. Cymbeline dried it off, but it no longer fits on his head so Vyruss carries it in his hand.

Tuwhit takes off to join Crusty. The eagle suggests, "Why don't you perch in the hawthorn tree instead? It is lower and closer to the flag. We must both keep fully alert. I don't trust the wizard's promises. I sent Maggie to spread the word around that all the other birds shall remain a good distance from the flag."

Gerald takes the Book of Lore out of the bag and shows it to Vyruss. He opens it to the right page and shows that to him also.

Vyruss smiles and nods. "Yes, it is indeed the same Book of Lore. I am satisfied there has been no attempt to secretly switch it."

With deep inner pain, Gerald kneels and uses his knee as a table. He places the valued book into the plastic bag, wraps it with the string, and ties it securely to protect it against possible damage. He does it reverently and solemnly. This is the history of his people and he, who has had charge over it, is permitting its loss. It is almost as though he is giving part of himself away. He is close to tears. *We are arming our enemy, who is so committed against us, with a most powerful weapon.*

Cydlo places his hand on Gerald's shoulder. The king feels the pain too. *Somehow, since the ambassador arrived this morning, I no longer have control over events. We are moving along on a course determined by the Wizard of Wozzle. Only he knows what the end of it all will be.* He sighs. *I trust my choice is the right one.*

Gerald is satisfied that the Book of Lore is weatherproof. He lifts the parcel to his lips in a silent good-bye and offers it to Vyruss who bows his head as he receives it. The ambassador looks to the king. "Are you ready?"

Solemnly, Cydlo nods his head. There is no joy on his face.

Gerald leaves them and joins Jock and the others waiting eighty paces back.

Rasputin lifts into the air. He is too small for those on the Brook side to see clearly at that distance. He flutters for a while and then settles back into the ash tree again. Something is happening on the Gyminge side. Beyonders discern nothing at all, but the birds and animals of the Brook, and the Twith and their tiny guests can see well enough.

Tuwhit sees best of all from his vantage point. He sees six tiny horses in pairs approaching. The pair at both front and rear are goblin cavalrymen carrying lances decorated with black pennants. The pair in the middle are clearly a woman and the Wizard of Wozzle. Tuwhit remembers him well from the battle at Squidgy's cottage a month ago. He is wearing the same clothes—a black hat and cloak and shiny black pointed shoes. The owl does not recognize the woman. The small cavalcade halts opposite the flag, which stirs only lazily as the breeze disturbs it into movement.

The four goblin soldiers dismount. Two hold the reins of the horses. A cavalryman assists the woman to dismount and another marches smartly forward towards the flag as though to seize hold of it. He comes to a sudden halt and bounces back. At this point, he is clear to all the watchers on the other side. He picks himself up, dusts himself off, reverses himself, and briskly marches back in the direction he came from. All who can see are counting. At forty paces, approximately, but not quite back to the grouped horses, he comes to a smart and abrupt halt. He stamps his heels as though he were on a parade ground rather than in a grassy meadow.

The wizard and his companion come and stand beside the stationary goblin. The man now continues his march a further sixty paces. Those who can, count. Each of his three companions leads a pair of horses and follows him. Again, a parade ground halt. He turns smartly and then, once the horses are behind him, stands at ease marking the hundred paces distance from the curtain.

The wizard raises his arm as a signal to the watchers on the other side of the curtain. Vyruss responds similarly before turning to the king with a questioning glance. He places his hat beside the marker pebble. The king does the same with his bouquet of rosebuds. Vyruss has the package. They walk forward together towards the black-and-white flag.

Plans Go Awry

The word *awry* is one of a group of words beginning with an *a*. Askew is another and so are agley, amiss, and asquint. They all mean roughly the same thing—things that cannot possibly go wrong because of the perfection of the planning that went into them, suddenly begin to display an unexpected flaw. It may only be a pinhole of error or oversight, but it expands at the speed of light to cause complete collapse.

There is a key piece of information that no one in the present planning process has any idea about. Lurking in the bracken, closer to the flag than anyone else, is a solitary, self-employed mercenary. A cold-blooded, cool and calculating, unblinking merchant-adventurer who would sell his mother to a maker of fur coats if the price was right. He thinks on his feet and can spring into action like a flash of lightning. Planners, no matter of what quality, stand little chance against an adversary such as Jacko. He is poised and waiting to pounce.

Vyruss and the king go forward together to the flag. Vyruss holds up the package so that the wizard can see it. He places it at the foot of the flag. Noticing that the mouth of the mole tunnel is still open, he kicks in several scoops of the soft, dark, fine earth. *I don't want any moles messing things up now. Another five minutes and the whole transaction will be concluded.* The king and the doctor walk back to their position and turn to face the flag.

On the other side, the queen is already moving forward to stand facing the package. She has no idea what the package contains. All she knows is that she is to gain her freedom in exchange for it. The wizard warned her, "Walk the last few paces with your hands held out in front of you in case there is an obstruction. You saw what happened to the cavalryman. I wouldn't wish that to happen to you."

From the distant molehill on the Brook, Elisheba recognizes her mother and gets excited. She waves, jumps up and down, and calls out, "Mummy, Mummy! It's me! Can you see me? I'm alive!"

Taymar holds on to her hand tightly lest she run forward and spoil what is happening.

The king also recognizes his wife. He twists the bouquet in his hands nervously and raises the flowers towards her, but stays where he is.

The queen stops as she reaches and touches the unseen curtain before her. As she takes her position opposite the Book of Lore, she sees her husband. A broad smile of pure joy envelops her face and she waves both hands over her head.

Vyruss is required to wait until the king recognizes the queen before he moves forward. He looks up at the king's beaming face.

Cydlo nods. "Yes, it is she. It is the queen surely enough. I thought I would never see the day."

This is the moment of awry, askew, agley, amiss, and asquint if not also absolute chaos all in one.

Even before Vyruss completes a first pace back to the curtain to stand alongside the Book of Lore, there is a flash of brown-and-tan low to the ground. It moves at the speed of a jetliner as it heads in the direction of the United States aiming to be there in less than five minutes. Passing by the flag with no slackening of momentum, the ferret snatches up the plastic-covered package. His prize catch dangles from his mouth as he swerves into the thick bracken and heads towards Africa.

Vyruss and the king break into a run forward. Behind them the Twith and the children charge forward also, shouting as they go.

Overhead, within a space of seconds, Tuwhit and Crusty are in frantic flight searching for any sign of movement beneath the bracken that will indicate the passage of Jacko. They see nothing. Maggie yells to the other magpies, "Alert all the other birds.

Quick!" The sky fills with birds as they get the news. They spread out wide in their search. Maggie turns and flies as fast as she can towards Squidgy's cottage. *Surely, that is where the ferret will be heading.*

Vyruss stands at the curtain looking towards the wizard. He waves his hands frantically. *Who is tricking whom? What is going on?*

Jacko has not only been recognized on the Brook side of the curtain, but Rasputin from his perch in the ash tree knows immediately and without doubt who it is that has spoiled the plan to gain possession of the Book of Lore. He flies back to the wizard and tells him excitedly, "It was that sneaky ferret who did this! The Twith are not playing tricks. Look at them. They are all in total confusion. Jacko acted alone. Boss, he's the one you have to deal with now, not the Twith rebels."

The wizard already knows. He too has seen and recognized the interfering predator. He takes a deep breath. "Yes, my friend, it means there is another party to bargain with, acting in his own interest. He is likely to prove very difficult. I've had dealings with the creature before. We better get across to Mrs. Squidge's cottage as soon as we can. If Jacko isn't there, we'll just wait for him to make the first move. He is likely to drive a hard bargain, and it will end up being most expensive."

The Twith are quite convinced that the wizard is involved in what just happened. This is obviously a strike coordinated by the master magician himself. They will not believe for one minute that he is innocent. Gerald cries out in anguish, "We've been tricked! We've fallen right into his trap of deceit. I don't blame Vyruss. He too has been tricked by the wizard. Our enemy has been brilliant. The only bait that could have brought the Book of Lore out into the open was the queen. Now he not only still has the queen, but he has the Book of Lore as well. What a fool I've been!"

Jock whistles for Tuwhit. He calls to Jordy and Barney, "Cum on. I' is time fur a showdown! We're goin' ta 'ead straight fur Squidgy's cottage. Th' SnuggleWump will be thur as well as th' teros, Cajjer, 'n' Squidgy. Nay matter. If th' ferre' is nay thur, we'll search 'im out. 'Urry up, Tuwhi'!"

Taymar recognizes what is happening. *I'm being left out! No deal, Jock! The Three Twithketeers are still the Three Twithketeers.* He kisses Elisheba and runs towards the owl who is just now landing. Barney quickly climbs on board, his catapult out and loaded. As Jordy starts to climb aboard, Taymar yells, "You can't go without me, Jock. We are in this together."

Jock nods agreement. Inwardly, he is glad to have someone of Taymar's strength and initiative alongside. Had there been time, they would have collected Ambro too, but there is no time to waste. They don't want to give the wizard an opportunity to get to Jacko before they do.

Tuwhit is into the air. Without gaining height, he flies as fast as he can over the croc' pond and down the cottage path. He knows where Jacko lives and will drop them at the entrance to Mole Hall.

Quite suddenly, behind them at the flag, the most surprising event of the whole afternoon occurs.

The queen, prompted by the unexpected instructions from the wizard behind her, steps forward. She feels the edge of an unseen curtain and steps through onto the Brook. The southerly breeze blows the full freshness of sea air—salt and all—straight into her face. It is like the perfume of roses she has only dreamed of. She is out of the silence of Gyminge into the chorus of birdsong and chatter. As she stumbles forward over the molehill, she falls into the arms of her husband who has run to meet her.

Vyruss, not understanding, tries to go through the other way according to the bargain that was made, but the curtain is closed tight. There is no sign of the wizard and his escort. Rasputin, too, is gone.

The Hunt for Jacko

The SnuggleWump has been continually disturbed since before dawn. Early on, it was the constant air traffic. He complains, "The cottage is getting to be as busy as the entrance to a beehive in high summer. It began with Mrs. Squidge and Cajjer taking off. The owl followed them and later the teros went into frantic flight. My mistress careened back into the house and then that pesky raven arrived again. Her cat—looking the worse for wear—straggled back shortly after." The SnuggleWump roars. "To play safe, I'm keeping my eyes red, although I have no idea what I'm supposed to be upset about."

There are strange noises inside the cottage that disturb him as well. He grumbles to himself. "Cajjer's tortured squeal is like the continuous high-pitched whine of a power line. It hurts my tender ears. Mrs. Squidge's groans have been at regular intervals like a doe rabbit having an endless litter of bunnies.

"Late in the afternoon, I saw two Little People, strangely clad and unknown to me, messing around at the foot of the porch steps. I'm fairly sure they are not goblins. Now they have gone into Mole Hall." The SnuggleWump is supersensitive to bad smells, especially that of the ferret. "I'm not sure those wee folk are going to like the smell in there, but I'm not going to make it any of my business.

"My association with Jacko is not particularly close. I get on better with the rabbits than I do with the ferret, so I occasionally tap them a warning when he's around. However, when the ferret went inside the cottage for a while, Mrs. Squidge was quieter and I was grateful for that. Now he's gone off towards the croc' pond, but I expect he'll be back down the path soon."

He sees the magpie that is usually perched high in the ash tree exploring close to ground level. She is searching for something, but doesn't find it. In the far distance, someone whistles shrilly. The bird disappears.

Next to disturb the SnuggleWump's day is the owl. He has cargo on his back. The SnuggleWump can see that the four passengers who tumble off are definitely Twith. They quickly disperse and the owl begins an irritating circling patrol close to the ground. Although the Little People are within reach, they are not bothering him and he intends to leave them alone. *I remember my encounter with them at the farmhouse and I'm not looking for a fight.* He is content to weave his two heads to and fro and show the extent of his teeth as though to let them know what he could do if he really became provoked.

Jordy and Taymar are close behind Jock to lend support. Jock has his dirk raised in his right hand. The other two search for and pick up from the ground sticks thick enough to knock each other's head off. A dozen paces further back, Barney has a stone in his catapult and the thick rubber is stretched to fire. He aims at the dark opening into the mole tunnel that leads to the croc' pond, in case Jacko should suddenly appear.

Tuwhit screeches to them from above. "There is another entrance into Mole Hall. I'll show you." Taymar and Jordy run off to the left following the owl.

The SnuggleWump roars again, louder. Both heads at once this time.

Jock can hear noises approaching from inside. He steps to the side of the entrance, ready to leap. To his utter amazement, two of the strangest Little People he has ever seen step out of Mole Hall holding their noses. They are carrying haversacks, but no weapons.

They look around, but do not see Jock. However, they see Barney. For a short moment, there is a pause for recognition and then they cheer with delight. They drop their haversacks and run towards him. They are clearly acquainted for the boy drops his catapult to his side and then lets it fall to the ground. He runs towards them and they hug each other, jumping up and down and ruffling each other's hair. They are speaking some foreign language.

Taymar and Jordy appear at the entrance into Mole Hall, as mystified as Jock at what they see. Jacko is clearly not inside although the place stinks of him. They are glad to be back out in the fresh air. Jordy sees Barney hugging two strangers and asks, "What on earth is going on here?"

Jock shrugs his shoulders. "I 'ave nay idea."

For a while, the SnuggleWump relaxes and lets his eyes turn orange and then green. Mrs. Squidge is unlikely to be watching and there's no one around to suggest he is slacking in his duties.

The two strangers have just been in the water somewhere. Their dark blue uniforms are wet, worn, and grubby. They are military uniforms, but the matching caps they wear are not dress caps—they are working caps. Both have medal ribbons. They offer their muddy hands in greeting to the three Twith.

Barney turns to Jock. "These are my friends. I haven't seen them for many years. Let's hide somewhere and I'll tell you all about them." He recovers his catapult and reloads.

Jock's main purpose in being anywhere near Squidgy's cottage is to recover the Book of Lore. He looks around and spots a likely place where they can be out of sight and yet watch for Jacko. "Le's go o'er thur, under th' porch steps. Tha' looks like a good place. We cun be in th' shadow o' th' stacked firewood." He whistles for Tuwhit. "Will ye go find ou' whether th' other searchers 'ave seen any sign o' Jacko on th' Brook?"

From within the house, accompanied by a high-pitched whine, comes an intermittent groaning like someone in pain. It's not so loud that it will seriously disturb them, although Jock is curious about it.

The SnuggleWump sighs and lowers first one head and then the other to the ground. He keeps an eye on the porch and the cottage door, but with all that moaning going on inside, he won't be surprised if supper isn't late tonight.

Barney introduces Otto, the taller of the pair, and then Klaus, plump and sporting a mustache. "It all happened a long while ago, long before Mrs. Squidge came to the Brook. At the time, the three of you were off in America while the rest of us stayed here in Smiler's cottage. Our entrance was a small tunnel right here at the foot of these porch steps, remember?"

All of the boy's audience are acquainted with the cottage and nod their heads. Even Otto and Klaus, although they are foreigners, appear to be following Barney's conversation easily.

"One day while I was out playing football with the rabbits, I spotted these same two Beyonders. They were full Beyonder-size and hiding in the brambles. Many villagers appeared to be searching the Brook to try and find them. Otto was sick and Klaus was trying to carry him and still keep him hidden. I abandoned my game and ran home to fetch Gerald. When we got back, we allowed them to see us. Like all other Beyonders, they were amazed to see Little People. Gerald offered to take care of the sick one who was vomiting. He also had an injured arm that looked as though it was broken. Klaus himself had cuts on his face and a black eye. Gerald warned them what would happen when they shrunk. He held out his hand to Klaus and I took hold of Otto's.

"DOINK! *WHOOSH!* In a flash, the two men were Little People also. Gerald and I hoisted and held Otto between us and took him back to the cottage. After several days, the searchers from the village abandoned their attempts to find them and quietly returned to the Brook. Cymbeline was a good nurse and Gerald carefully dispensed medicines and herbs. Otto's forearm was indeed broken and Gerald fixed it rigidly with splints while it slowly mended. There was plenty of room with the three of you away and, equally important to the two starving men, plenty of food. Why don't you tell your side of the story now?"

Otto appears to be the spokesman for the pair and his English is more fluent. "We are from Germany. Our country was at war with England. We are pilots and our plane crashed over near Stanford. We swung to earth below our parachutes and tried to avoid being captured. For several days, we hid in the woods, but then we were seen and a search began to find us. We were almost without food since we landed although Klaus managed to steal some eggs, which we ate raw.

"Our aim was to get back to Germany safely without being put into a prison camp for the remainder of the war. There was no hope of escaping capture as Beyonders. We decided to remain the size of the Twith. That offered us safety in travel. We hoped we could find our way to an airfield or onto a ship in Dover and smuggle ourselves back to Europe. We would sort out the problem of returning to Beyonder-size once we were back home. We figured that for every problem, there is an answer, and for sure, we would find it."

OTTO AND KLAUS

For all Little People, time is different than it is for Beyonders. It passes at a different speed and changes occur at a different rhythm. The two fugitives think the war is still in progress.

Otto continues their story. "We are tired of being in hiding. It is a struggle just to survive. Will the war never end? There is no one to talk to except ourselves. We have no idea what is happening in the world we left. Summer has followed winter and winter has followed summer on and on and on. We not only went to Dover but to the ports of Ramsgate and Manston as well. Although sometimes we thought we were close to crossing the Channel, we never succeeded.

"We haven't found a way to enlarge ourselves back to our normal size. We are nervous about that. Maybe there won't be anyone in Germany who knows how to do it either. We don't want to end up in a shoebox as sideshow freaks in Stuttgart. So we decided to come back to the Brook and find one of our four Twith friends. And we have! We will let you return us to our original size and then we will surrender to the English authorities. We'll take our punishment, serve our time, and wait until we are released when the war is over. It will happen sometime. As civilians, we are going to open an English pub in Berlin with a fish and chip bar as specialty food. We'll offer special discounts and free vinegar for all Luftwaffe prisoners of war."

Jordy interrupts, "I think you should know that the war ended over fifty years ago. You don't need to worry about being imprisoned. You can just plan your future."

Great smiles wreath the faces of both Otto and Klaus. Otto continues, "It has been months since we made this decision. We had to find our way back to Smiler's cottage. It was a long march retracing our steps and it wasn't easy. Once we arrived in Sellindge, we still had to find and reach the Brook. It has taken us two days to get across Walker's field. Then, when we once again recognized familiar territory, we again had to be very careful.

"Just a short while ago, within the last hour, we were almost in big trouble. We sat down for a rest on a dry clump of marsh grass and were nearly knocked over by a weasel or a stoat or a polecat. We didn't know what it was, but it was much bigger than we are. It could have gobbled us up in one or two mouthfuls, and that would have put an end forever to the dreams of a fish and chip bar in Berlin. We ducked into the floating weeds behind a clump of grass and waited a long while before slowly raising our heads.

"The brown-and-tan creature was just ahead of us. He had skidded to a halt near the only bright purple spotted marsh orchid we had seen on the bog. We were using it as a marker and walking towards it. All the others were white or pink or red or mixtures of those colors. The animal didn't see us, but began digging in the dirt near the plant. He had something in his mouth he was burying. It didn't look like it was a cache of food. It was something else. He pushed back the dirt and then raised his head and looked around. Fortunately, he did not look in our direction. There were many birds in the air, but few of them were over the bog. They were mostly to the east of the bog. The odd creature waited a moment or so and then sneaked quickly and carefully away towards Brook Lane and Walker's field."

The Twith Logue have been listening in rapt silence. Jock is the first to speak. "Cun ye take us ta this purple spotted marsh orchid?"

Klaus does not answer the question but asks, with a questioning smile, "Why?"

Jock doesn't want to spend time on explanations, but it looks as though he is going to have to.

Taymar knows what Jock is thinking and he knows what to do. There is no need to wait for instructions. He gets up, slips away from the others, and walks quickly along the path towards the croc' pond. He whistles for Tuwhit. The bird will hear that call from among a thousand others. His ear is tuned for it, and he has no trouble distinguishing it from all the multitude of sounds that fill the air.

Taymar explains quickly to the bird. "Somewhere close by here on the bog is a purple spotted marsh orchid. I want you to go find it. It is the only one of its color among reds, pinks, and whites. There will be no mistaking it. There will be signs of digging beside it. That's where Jacko buried the Book of Lore.

"Just guard the area so that Jacko doesn't come back for the Book of Lore before we get there. I'll whistle for you again as soon as we can get Klaus or Otto to come with us. It may take a few minutes yet."

The bird is away like a flash, and Taymar, walking slowly to avoid disturbing the snoozing SnuggleWump, resumes his place with the others.

Jock knows what Taymar went to do; they have worked together as a team for centuries. He is being patient in his explanations to Otto and Klaus. He already tried to explain the flight from Gyminge of the seven Twith and their refuge in Smiler's cottage. But the German boys have trouble understanding his Scottish dialect. He turns to Taymar. "Why don't ye tell them 'bout th' Book o' Lore?"

Taymar explains, "The Wizard of Wozzle is anxious to obtain our Book of Lore because it contains all the traditions of our people. He captured the wife of our king and is holding her as a hostage. He proposed to us only this morning that we exchange our Book of Lore for our queen. He suggested that the queen and the Book of Lore be placed either side of an invisible curtain that would separate them. Everyone else would stand back at least forty paces. We agreed, although with misgivings. We were all in position and expecting the exchange to occur as he had said. Suddenly, his ferret, which you mistook for a stoat or polecat, rushed out of hiding and seized the Book of Lore in his mouth and was gone before we could even sneeze. We didn't expect such vicious trickery, although we should have known that the wizard cannot be trusted.

"Now he has both the Book of Lore and the queen. What you have just told us gives us hope that we can yet retrieve the situation. Certainly, the Book of Lore is what the ferret just buried near the purple spotted marsh orchid, and if we can get there before he returns, we are at least back where we started. Will you help us?"

Klaus looks across at Otto and smiles. "No, I don't think we will take you to the purple spotted marsh orchid. But kindly answer us another question. Is it within your power to restore us to full-size—the size we used to be?"

Jock is troubled by what he hears. *Why won't they 'elp in th' recovery o' th' Book o' Lore?* "Aye, I culd do so now, righ' a' this momen', if ye shuld so wish."

"Kindly do so to my friend Otto. Otto, pass me your haversack to hold."

Jock smiles anxiously at the taller stranger. "Ye 'ad better cum out frum under th' steps or ye will bang yur 'ead. Now, cross yur two fingers like this." Jock demonstrates with his own fingers.

Otto obediently crosses his fingers.

"Now 'old me 'and."

Otto reaches out and catches hold. In the farmhouse, this happens several dozen times each day as the children exchange sizes. It is no different with Otto. DOINK! *WHOOSH!* Everything around shrinks as Otto zooms up like a rocket bound for the sky. He suddenly stops zooming, takes a deep breath, and looks down to where his tiny friend is waving.

Klaus turns grinning to Jock. "Well done. I'm next, but before that it is your turn. I said we will not take you to the purple spotted marsh orchid for there is simply no need. There is nothing there. We ourselves looked to see what the ferret had hidden before we came on to the cottage. Look in Otto's haversack."

At the top of the haversack, as Jock opens it, is a muddy little package—a plastic shopping bag tied with string to render it waterproof. Long before the bag is opened and its contents checked, Jock knows that everything is all right after all.

Klaus holds out his hand. His fingers are crossed.

Jock smiles. There is a lump in his throat and tears in his eyes. He has trouble saying, "Thank ye," as he reaches out his hand.

DOINK! *WHOOSH!* Klaus is full Beyonder-size once again. "Thanks, Jock. It's an entirely different perspective from up here. But it's good to be back to size. We'll never forget you."

Barney and the Three Twithketeers wave cheerily as their German friends depart. Jock's kilt flares up and out as he breaks into dancing the Highland Fling, hands arched over his head. Barney tries to join in, but can't spin as fast as Jock. He whirls his catapult above his head. Jordy and Taymar stand with arms folded watching with amusement. All four are relaxed and happy. The Book of Lore has been recovered. Once again, the wizard's trickery has been foiled.

WHO'S BOOK OF LORE?

As Tuwhit carries the four elated adventurers from the cottage back to the rendezvous point, Barney has the honor of holding the Book of Lore. It is tight to his chest. The owl flies low.

Across to their left and higher in the sky, two ravens heading south fly alongside each other. Rasputin's twisted flight is easy to recognize. The other bird will be the triumphant wizard on his way to Squidgy's cottage to collect the Book of Lore from Jacko and celebrate his success with Mrs. Squidge.

At the rendezvous point, they expect to see the children helping the Twith to search the bracken and a disconsolate king and brokenhearted princess needing encouragement. That is not what they find. There is no one there! Tuwhit circles slowly near where the flag was fluttering. The flag is gone and all the Little People have disappeared, presumably back home. One or two Beyonder-size strangers in the distance are exercising their dogs near Cope farm, but surely, their presence would not have scared the Little People back to the farmhouse. Beyond the curtain, no sign remains of any activity in Gyminge.

There is no point in landing. Although they have no idea why it has happened, there are only a few very cautious rabbits and some badgers around. Tuwhit heads for the farmhouse and lands lightly on the top of the well cover. He looks up to the roof. Crusty is back standing on the chimney slab. He has relieved the sparrow hawk and the kestrel on guard duty. He kaa's a greeting, watches them unload, and waits for the owl to come up and join him. He seems less worried and restless than the loss of the Book of Lore would be expected to cause.

There are balloons and decorations around the front entrance into Twith Mansion. A big sign bears the marks of Gerald's expertise in calligraphy.

Welcome to the Brook, Queen Sheba

Taymar expresses what the others are thinking. "Ah, you should have saved your energy, Gerald! At least, the children will enjoy the cakes and sandwiches prepared for the celebration."

Jordy voices his thoughts. "Now that the wizard's trickery has been exposed, surely any thought of the exchange will have been dropped for good. What would have been an absolute calamity has been averted only by the most fortunate encounter with Otto and Klaus. We'll have a lot to tell the others. Gerald, for one, will be grateful for the retrieval of the Book of Lore."

Jock has an urgent word with Tuwhit. "I wan' ye ta go keep watch fur th' wizard a' th' cottage. Cum le' me know if 'e leaves 'n' where 'e goes."

Taymar, anxious to find and console Elisheba over the collapse of the negotiations and the failure to recover her mother, is first into Twith Mansion. He races past Buffo with just a brief, "Hi, Buffo." He hurries down the hall, followed by the three others.

Barney is looking for Gerald. He wants to surprise him. The large living room is empty, but there are noises of jubilation coming from upstairs. Now it is Barney who is surprised. "Jubilation? What's going on? This is the strangest of days! Is it a birthday we overlooked? What is there to laugh about?"

Taymar wastes no time in the mansion and runs up the stairs to the Inglenook fireplace hearth. He finds a party going on! A radiant Elisheba spots him standing at the staircase entrance and runs to throw herself into his arms. Recovering her balance, she grabs him by his hand and pulls him into the center of the hearth. She has never looked so happy or so beautiful.

"Mummy, here's Taymar and I love him so much! Taymar, I want you to meet my mother, Queen Sheba. For the first time in centuries, all my family are together and I am so happy. I think this is the happiest day of my life! If only Nettie could be here too, it would be perfect."

When Elisheba pauses for breath, Taymar, taken totally by surprise, bows happily to the unexpected mother of his bride. Her resemblance to her daughter is uncanny. Their features are so similar. She too, even though tired from her long journey, looks gloriously happy. He recognizes the dress she wears as one of Elisheba's. His bride-to-be puts her arm around Taymar's waist and swings him around and around in a few dancing steps of absolute bliss. The young man has to adjust his mood, but he does so quickly and responds to Elisheba's joy with his own. From the dismay of five o'clock on the Brook to exhilaration on the farmhouse hearth in less than two hours! Whatever explanations are called for can wait.

The pair are not on their own in their happiness. Spontaneously things are happening all around. Cymbeline and Ambro are dancing exuberantly, matching themselves as far as they can to Taymar and Elisheba. Even Cydlo is on his feet dancing with the queen. He is dancing very smoothly for one still recovering from a leg injury. He looks as though he has suddenly shed years off his age.

While everyone was out, Gumpa and gran'ma prepared the tea and sweet refreshments. The children have been busy partaking of the goodies at the table, but are now shrinking back to partying size as quickly as they can. They don't want to miss out on any of the fun. Stumpy, on a three-legged stool, holds out his hand to any children looking to shrink. As usual, Jared, the grandson from Texas, looks like being the last to finish eating. Not because he is slow, but because he is sampling twice as much of everything as anyone else.

Specs with his harmonica, and Bajjer with his recorder, are making music to dance by. The Shadow children are playing

Punjabi rhythms using their hands or serving spoons on the pots at the back of the hearth. Bimbo is working the fire tongs.

Barney spots Gerald and presents him with the recovered package. He doesn't wait to explain to the startled seer where it has come from. He spots Ginger and dashes over to stand opposite her where they go into the frantic head jerking, body twisting, and jumping gyrations that he has seen Bajjer attempting when he dances with Stormy. He has been practicing by himself in his bedroom when Stumpy is elsewhere. Ginger is no less active and frantic than he. The other children are also finding this activity more to their taste than the formal styles and slow footwork of their elders. Titch, the sweet young granddaughter from Texas, is playing a game of survival with Micah. They are balancing precariously on one of the antique, cylindrical, stoneware, hot water bottles lying on its side. With all their wild contortions, it seems certain that one of them is going to slip off soon.

Over near the coal scuttle, gran'ma is guiding Gumpa into a slow waltz without recognizable accompaniment. It has little relation to the activity going on around them but is about the best her husband can manage. When Jock asks gran'ma for a dance, she shows what she can really do when she is not held back. Jock is matched step for step and whirls faster and yet faster to outpace his partner. She is with him all the way. Gumpa is happy to rest and watch his wife enjoying herself.

Stumpy whispers to Nick that he has a couple of homemade stringed instruments in the back cupboard of his workshop that also make music. The grandson from Idaho is excited. He plays the guitar and has his own band back in Idaho. He races off upstairs and comes down with instruments resembling a zither and a banjo. Stumpy takes the zither and begins strumming the strings. Nick is soon plucking music from the banjo.

Dr. Vyruss Tyfuss has by this time been fully welcomed into the Twith family. The return of the queen has broken down all barriers. His dismay at the capture of the Book of Lore by the streaking Jacko has been clear to all. He has had no part in it. Any hesitations the Twith might have had about letting him know about Elisheba or Ambro have been forgotten.

Vyruss has a fine tenor voice and he knows well the catchy tune, Hornpipe, from *Water Music* by Handel that Stumpy is playing. He appoints himself orchestra conductor and choir director and principal soloist. Slowly, he groups all the musicians together, bringing them shuffling into the corner of the fireplace. He picks up a toothpick that rolled off the table and uses it as his baton to guide his choir into following the quick rhythm of the music that Stumpy is playing.

Outside, Buffo listens with interest to the tenor soloist and determines to find out who it is. He smiles to himself. *That soloist will give me a definite advantage over Bingo for the wedding music.*

Off by himself in the other corner of the fireplace and blissfully happy is Gerald. He wonders, *How can it be that Jock and the others recovered this grubby little package?* He loosens the string and peeks inside to be absolutely sure no switch has taken place. *As soon as an opportunity arises, I want to slip off downstairs and return the Book of Lore to the hiding place where it rightfully belongs. I'll ask Jordy to come down with me as soon as he pauses in his dancing with Margaret. I can get the full story from him.* Since the pairs are forming up to do the Highland Fling and Jock is exchanging his partner for Jordy's, it may take a while before the Book of Lore is safely tucked away once more.

It is then that a staggering thought comes to the seer. *Who does the Book of Lore belong to now that we have Queen Sheba?*

Gerald hopes there is a way out, but in his heart, he already knows the answer.

TRUTH WILL OUT!

The motto of the Twith Logue is "Truth Will Out!" These are the words that Jock, masquerading as the wounded King Rufus of Gyminge, shouted as the eagle carried six Little People over the lake and away from the castle to the Beyond.

Truth has been their watchword ever since. Dayko warned them in the Rime.

> *Forget not the land that you leave*
> *As you flee from the pain and grief.*
> *Let Truth in your heart ever burn,*
> *It alone can bring your Return.*

The old seer is quite clear in what he says, and Gerald knows that he has no choice but to keep to it. Without truth in their hearts, there will be no Return.

None of them have ever questioned what Dayko said. In Gyminge, they were taught from childhood to always tell the truth no matter what the consequences might be. Since their escape, the Twith have been especially careful to avoid the trap of untruthfulness. They all know that staying truthful at all times is essential to ensure their return home. There have been many times when they needed to be extra sensitive to the situation and stay alert. Often, it was better to stay silent than risk speaking a half-truth. Exaggeration had to be eliminated from their conversation. Over the centuries, the habit of complete truthfulness has been confirmed and become rooted within them.

All seven of them have constantly guarded their words and their thoughts. In the early days, alert and watchful, they used to check and correct each other, but the habit of truthfulness has so steadily grown within each of them that for a long while there has been no need for reminders. Truth has become an inseparable part of their nature.

The Twith have been concerned about their helpers from the Beyond. Dayko is not clear about what would happen if one of the Beyonders should tell a lie. But they have urged each of the children to keep to the same standard of truth that they follow themselves. Deceit is a contagion that spreads like a disease if it is not checked.

They have also known that should the wizard ever become aware of Dayko's Rime, he would immediately be alerted to his simplest and his most powerful weapon. Tricking or persuading even just one of the Twith into untruthfulness could become an insurmountable wall that prevents their return to Gyminge. That would mean perpetual banishment in the Beyond for them.

Gerald is perceptive and realizes that this is what could now be happening! The matter needs an early resolution before the situation gets out of control. He needs in particular to share his concerns with both King Rufus and Jock. He recalls words Dayko taught him long ago.

> *Better not*
> *To achieve worthy goals*
> *Than to achieve them*
> *By unworthy means.*

Throughout the evening, the music careens along its merry journey. There are pauses for refreshments and then a diversion into skits prepared for an earlier occasion. He watches Jock and Cydlo and Taymar finding ever new reserves of energy to match the other younger ones around them. While cocoa is being prepared, Jordy performs a few conjuring tricks. The new High Seer looks at the radiant faces of gran'ma and Queen Sheba, the two younger brides-to-be, the children, the other Twith and shudders.

Gerald thoughtfully studies his ink-stained fingers. "I fear that the wizard has tricked us and wins after all." He straightens up, filled with sharp determination. "We must act quickly to prevent that. If we fail to do so, the Return will be only a dream and never a reality. The issue is simple. We entered into a binding agreement with the wizard. The king accepted the wizard's proposal for an exchange on the terms and conditions that the wizard set down. A simple exchange of the Book of Lore for the queen. The king and Jock and I each separately agreed there would be no change in the Lore before the time of its exchange for the queen.

"Had the wizard broken his pledge to release the queen, things would be different. He could very well have done so for there were a few moments when all the options were with him. If that had happened and the wizard had played false, then we would have been released from our part of the agreement. However, the wizard proved his cunning and outwitted us. He saw in a flash where he could gain the advantage. He kept his part of the bargain. He released the queen, who has little value to him save as a hostage. By doing so, he placed the Twith in his debt until the exchange is actually completed. He has as good as placed handcuffs on us.

"The Book of Lore does not belong to the Twith any more. It belongs to the wizard. He fulfilled his part of the bargain. With the Book of Lore in our possession, we are the ones who failed to keep our promise. It does not matter whether the wizard is aware of the ferret's plan to grab the Book of Lore or not. He may have had two plans in case one should go wrong. That doesn't make any difference anyway. He has kept his part of the bargain and we have failed to keep ours."

Gerald knows he must wait until the festivities are over to proceed, but to him it is clear. "There is only one thing we can do. Grieve as we might, we must send the Book of Lore to the wizard without delay. If possible, Dr. Tyfuss should be on his way tonight."

Gran'ma indicates to Jock that it is time to draw the evening to an end. "It's getting late and I need to get my charges restored to full-size so we can have devotions and send then off to bed."

She has the weddings on her mind. *Time is running out. It's only two days to the weddings. I really wish we had time to sew a new dress for Queen Sheba, but I just don't think that is going to be possible. The events of this day have totally overtaken my arrangements for Taymar and Ambro to have a bachelor party with their friends. And I wanted to have bridal showers for Elisheba and Cymbeline. Maybe we can squeeze those in tomorrow, but it's doubtful. I'm determined we're not going to miss out on the rehearsal dinner though. The rehearsal is as essential to the wedding as the ceremony itself. Well, almost. That's tomorrow night with a dinner afterwards. Jock and Gumpa will be the effective hosts.* Neither Gumpa nor Jock has any idea what is coming or that this is to be their responsibility.

Jock acknowledges gran'ma's request. He whispers to Specs, "Do nay star' a new burst o' dancin' 'til I 'ave a chance ta speak." Slowly, the music winds down. At last, the final percussions stop. The king, who has found more energy than he knew he possessed, looks curiously towards Jock. *Surely, the evening is early yet? I'm really enjoying myself. This is a very, very special occasion.*

Jock holds up his hands. "Please sit righ' where ye are. Gran'ma says i' is time fur th' children ta put an end ta thur celebrations. She feels i' is time fur devotions and bed."

There is a lot of violent headshaking and some audible, good-natured dissent.

"Gran'ma 'as imminent weddings ta perpare fur so we mus' excuse 'er 'n' th' children. 'Owe'er, fur ye 'n' yur wife, Cydlo, this is an importan' occasion 'n' we wuld be loathe ta end 'til ye feel ready. We ask fur yur counsel whether we shuld continue."

Before Cydlo can respond, Jock continues, "I also 'ave sum joyful news ta share with all o' ye. Th' Book o' Lore which we saw Jacko take this afternoon 'as been recovered in a mos' remarkable way! We cun rejoice tha' wha' was los' 'as been found."

There is awestruck silence. Gerald is on his feet holding up the package for all to see. The room erupts with the sounds of clapping and shouting of "Hurrah!" Stumpy plucks at his zither, thumping his good foot and making up a song of four line verses on the spur of the moment, rhyming Lore with or, more, sore, poor, war, score, for, door, floor... The verses are rolling out.

No one is yet ready for bed. Gran'ma has totally forgotten about bedtime for the children and is leading the snaking line doing the Hokey Pokey. She is twisting her hips and making as much noise as anyone else.

As Jock joins the line, he catches Gerald's urgent whisper. "Jock, I need to see you right away, downstairs. Please bring Cydlo."

GIVE UP THE BOOK OF LORE?

Upstairs the revelries continue. Gerald asked Jordy to ensure that no one else comes down to join them for a while so the evening festivities on the hearth take their noisy course.

The three men sit at the dining table. With them is Queen Sheba who is unwilling to lose her husband's company so soon after being reunited with him. She sits next to the king and squeezes his hand as though needing to be sure he is really there. Between them on the worn oak surface of the table is the Book of Lore.

Gerald has removed it from the plastic bag and is grateful to see that it is undamaged after its various adventures. He very briefly shares why he has called them together. "It is my opinion that the Book of Lore needs to be taken without delay to the wizard."

Eyebrows raise, but no one breaks in with questions.

"We are bound, not only by our traditions and honor, but by the admonition of Dayko's Rime as well, to keep our commitment to give the Book of Lore to the wizard in exchange for the queen."

Queen Sheba listens with great care. Dayko's Rime is new to her. Cydlo has told her of the negotiations between himself and the wizard for her release in exchange for the Book of Lore. She was surprised and pleased when he told her that all the free Twith concurred in the exchange. She holds her peace for the time being. She knows she will have her opportunity to share her thoughts and feelings in due course.

The king does not respond immediately although his look is grave. Instead, he turns to Jock and asks, "How was the Book of Lore recovered?" He has no knowledge of Mrs. Squidge's cottage except by hearsay and occasionally he asks questions to clarify his mental pictures.

Jock relates the meeting with Otto and Klaus and the successful retrieval of the Book of Lore.

The king comments, "I wonder whether Otto and Klaus and their remarkable appearance at just the right moment to observe Jacko hiding the Book of Lore wasn't just coincidence, but part of an uncanny pattern of pre-ordered events where a higher power is at work. It is almost as though we are musicians in an orchestra. Only the conductor can hear the harmony each of his performers is helping to create as he directs their playing."

Jock goes on to explain. "As we returned ta th' flag rendezvous point, two ravens flew across th' bog in th' other direction. One was clearly Rasputin; 'is style o' flyin' is unmistakable. Almos' certainly th' other was th' wizard. They were goin' lickety-spli' fur Squidgy's cottage. Tuwhi' is thur keepin' watch, bu' so far thur is nay word tha' th' wizard lef'. Presumably, 'e is still a' th' cottage."

The king knows in his heart that Gerald is right, but he won't admit it just yet. "What are your thoughts, Gerald, as to how the Book of Lore might be returned to the wizard…if that is what we decide to do?"

"We have the wizard's ambassador here, Cydlo. Dr. Tyfuss represents the wizard and is authorized to act for him. I believe that we shall have kept our word when we place the Book of Lore in the hands of the ambassador. It is up to us to assist him on his way as far as the waterfall. But then, he must determine the action he wishes to take from that point onward."

Cydlo next turns to ask Jock a question, but Queen Sheba lays her hand on his arm. "May I please say something?" The smiling nod of assent encourages her to speak. She looks at her husband with eyes brimming with love. "There is, I think, perhaps an alternative you might consider. Although the wizard is a master of trickery, we can't be certain whether there was trickery in this instance. The agreement in the form in which it was made failed at the very moment that the ferret stole the Book of Lore. He broke the agreement for both of you. The agreement you made became impossible for either of you to comply with. From that moment, it was no longer binding on either you or the wizard. But there is another way to maintain our integrity. We can go back to the original position before the agreement was broken.

"Instead of giving the Book of Lore to the wizard, let me return into captivity in Gyminge. He cannot take away from me all that I've experienced this past few hours. I can savor for years, even for centuries, what I just received. I can wait, my darling, with great peace for you to come, and I know you will. I will dream of our lovely daughter and her happiness. I will recall with joy and gratitude the wonderful young people I have met here today. I will remember Jock and his friends. If the wizard places me back in the bottle until you come, that will mean nothing to me. He cannot take my memories away. These will always stay with me and encourage my waiting hours."

Before the king can respond, Gerald raises his hand. He is very concerned about the argument the queen just put forward. "Sire, with all due respect to the queen, I believe that our agreement was based upon an exchange and not upon the manner in which the exchange might be effected. We all concurred with your decision that the Book of Lore should be exchanged for the queen.

"Had we not been able to recover the Book of Lore from the ferret, we would not have argued over the way Jacko interfered in the exchange. Feeling that we had kept our side of the bargain, we would have happily left the wizard to sort matters out with the ferret. But now, I cannot feel we are in a position to go back to the beginning even if we could accept the sacrifice of herself that the queen offers."

Jock has been silent. Integrity has strange twists. The little Scot has always tried to govern his actions and responses by what is right. He shares his thoughts. "Wha' is th' message fur th' Twith in this situation? So far we 'ave acted with complete faithfulness. Now, by a strange series o' unplanned events we 'ave possession o' both th' Book o' Lore 'n' th' queen. We are th' victors in a bargain where th' intention was thur wuld nay be either victor or loser. If th' wizard were in our shoes, 'e wuld undoubtedly consider this a complete victory o'er 'is enemies. Bu' we are nay th' wizard.

"Cydlo, Gerald is righ'. We gave our word 'n' we mus' keep i'. We recognized earlier that' i' wuld be grievous ta give up th' Book o' Lore. 'Owe'er, we accepted tha' risk then 'n' mus' do so agin. Th' queen's suggestion ta return ta captivity isn't an option which releases us frum our promise ta th' wizard. We cun nay delay in sendin' th' ambassador back ta Gyminge with th' Book o' Lore. Th' choice is yours ta make 'n' we shall support tha' choice wha'e'er i' is, bu' this is wha' I think we mus' do."

Cydlo nods. "Gerald, will you please ask the ambassador if he will come down and talk with us? We need to get him on his way at once." Beneath the table, the queen is holding his hand tight and gives a squeeze. She has tried.

VYRUSS RETURNS TO GYMINGE

The party upstairs continues as vigorously as ever. The ambassador, despite his tendency to be flatfooted and a tad overweight, is an accomplished dancer with natural rhythm. His female partners seem ready to try any kind of dance. With so many of the boys making music, the girls trade off partners as they spin around the floor. They seem to have even more energy than the boys.

Just now, Stormy is the one waltzing with Vyruss. As he twirls her under his arm, both her skirt and her brown ponytail are caught up in the action. As he brings her back into his arms, he shares his thoughts with her. "I have rarely enjoyed myself so much. This is even better than watching woodlouses. I'm glad I didn't need to surrender myself as hostage for the queen. She just passed through the curtain onto the Brook and into the arms of her husband. I was delighted to hear Jock's announcement about the recovery of the Book of Lore. There is no question that the Twith have gained the victory over the wizard. The magician's plans have collapsed around him. When I return to the castle, I will report exactly what happened and wait for a response. Hopefully, I won't be held personally responsible for the failure of this particular mission. After all, both Rasputin and the wizard himself were close enough to see what happened. It was totally outside of my control. There will doubtless be fireworks, but surely, they will be directed at Jacko. Now that he can't produce the Book of Lore, any negotiations with the ferret are bound to fail. No doubt the wizard's fertile mind will soon be scheming some other devious plan."

Gerald taps him on the shoulder. "Cydlo wants you downstairs."

Vyruss releases Stormy. "Excuse me, I must leave you stranded. Sorry." He follows Gerald downstairs.

King Rufus asks him to sit and explains, "The situation concerning the Book of Lore has been carefully considered. These Twith elders believe that they are committed to keeping their side of the bargain with the wizard. They feel they have an obligation to be sure the Book of Lore gets into the hands of the wizard as quickly as possible. I concur with their decision. Dr. Tyfuss, as representative of the wizard, we are handing over to you the copy of the Book of Lore that was recovered from where the ferret hid it. Will you kindly verify that the Book of Lore Gerald now offers to you for your inspection is in fact the same unblemished volume that you saw earlier?"

Vyruss thoughtfully picks up the treasured volume. "Yes, of course. This is the same book I examined earlier." He is puzzled. "Why would you give up possession of this book now? You clearly have ended with an advantage. You not only have the queen, but the Book of Lore as well."

"Gerald is guided by Dayko's Rime. The ancient seer warned that only truth will allow the Return of the Twith to their homeland. By keeping both the book and the queen, they would be breaking the agreement they made with the wizard. That would be deceitful and the same as telling a lie. It is imperative that we release the Book of Lore to the wizard. To the best of our knowledge, he is still at Mrs. Squidge's. If you wish, you can deliver the Book of Lore to him at the cottage rather than back in Gyminge. Otherwise, it will be wise and prudent and right that you return to Gyminge immediately and place the Book of Lore in the hands of the wizard when he returns. The owl has been sent for to transport you either to the cottage or to the bog. Buffo has also been alerted to stand by to take you across the bog to the waterfall if you decide to return to Gyminge instead of going to the cottage."

The ambassador gulps. *The Twith are throwing away a glorious victory! They have won the battle of the bargain hands down, ending up with both trophies. Now, merely to keep their word and for no other more pressing reason, they are going to throw their gains away! They can be quite sure the wizard will take full advantage of their weakness and their scruples. This is not the way to win either battles or wars. Well, at least I can delay things a little to help the Twith in spite of themselves. After all, I really am on their side. No need to make it easy for the wizard. Until the magician gets back to Gyminge, he's not going to have any chance to read the Lore.*

He sighs. "I'll miss the company and I'll miss the party. If the owl and Buffo will return me to the waterfall, that will be fine. I hope to see you again shortly, although that will depend on State business. Meanwhile, I wish you all well in the weddings about to take place. I'm sorry I won't be present, but I recognize that I must indeed be on my way without delay. I trust your plans for the summer prosper. Jock, will you please extend to the company upstairs my apologies for leaving so abruptly without farewells?"

Gerald carefully rewraps the inspected Book of Lore in the plastic shopping bag and reties it with string. He places the package in a black satchel and puts that in a big plastic bag. Rolling the top edges down, he ties the far ends together in a knot. With a heavy sigh, he hands it over to Vyruss.

After farewells, the king and his queen, still holding hands, go back upstairs. The children have been wanting to hear the queen's story and she has promised to tell them, though it may be in installments. Jock and Gerald accompany Vyruss outside. Rain threatens but has not yet begun. Crusty swoops down from the chimney to check who has come out and swings back out of sight again.

While they wait for Tuwhit beside the sycamore tree, Jock encourages the ambassador. "Be ready a' any momen' fur news tha' we are on our way. We will move as quickly as we are able. We will try ta locate ye as soon as we arrive in Gyminge. Remember, ye mus' stick ta th' truth if ye are goin' ta be able ta 'elp yur people free themselves frum th' grasp o' th' wizard."

Tuwhit soars in with a *swoosh* and shares the news from the cottage. "The wizard and Jacko are in the bedroom upstairs. Jacko must already have been inside the cottage before I arrived. The curtains were pulled soon after the bedroom lights went on and they are still on. Rasputin is waiting on the ridge, but he is at the opposite end from the teros. Those creatures seem to be in a state of shock and are all huddled closely together. The SnuggleWump's eyes are green. The cottage porch is empty. There is groaning and a strange high-pitched whine coming from downstairs. Neither Squidgy nor Cajjer has been outside while I've been watching. Both sparrows, Sparky and her brother, will stay on guard duty until I return."

The owl squats low. All three of the Little People get on his back. Jock and Gerald are going to take a quick turn around the Brook and over Squidgy's cottage after they drop off the doctor. It is midevening and near midsummer so the light is still good as he takes off.

Upstairs in the cottage, Jacko is on the floor, leaning against the bedroom door with his paws behind his head. The wizard's pillow supports his back. Mrs. Squidge has painfully brought up a tray of tea with two cups and a plate of watercress sandwiches. She filled another plate with all the cold sausages she was keeping in the pantry for her own consumption. Jacko has eaten them all. Only crumbs remain.

The ferret and the wizard are close to concluding their negotiations. Jacko considers that this is a discussion among equals— two businessmen sorting out a deal for their mutual advantage. "Well, Griswold, it is plain that people like yourself can get hold of pocket watches with gold chains by just going into a shop and purchasing them. However, that is not possible for a ferret like myself. My kind would get short shrift in the Ashford market. They would probably have the dogs set on us. We have no choice. We have to wait until one of our human friends sees our desperate need to be able to tell the time and gives us a spare one of their own. Without being able to tell the time, how can two friends ever reach a deal that depends on perfect timing as well as mutual trust and advantage? Now, if I were able to tell the time, I would know at once whether there is enough time and light left to be able to discover the place where I hid the Book of Lore. Otherwise, it might have to be put off until morning. Who knows whether the terms of the deal would be the same after each of us has had a good night's sleep and opportunity to think about it?"

The wizard sadly unbuttons from his waistcoat pocket his watch. It is one that he has had since he was a librarian in King Druthan's castle over a thousand years ago. Reluctantly, he hands his treasured timepiece to Jacko.

Jacko is effusive in his praise. "Now there's real friendship for you! I am full of admiration for the quality of your friendship. I appreciate and treasure it. Where else would I meet such unexpected generosity?" He twirls his new possession by the chain and looks at it upside down. "Yes, I think there is still time." He looks out the window at the sky. "Surely, there is enough light."

The wizard thinks disgustedly. *Of course, there is. There's a good three hours of daylight left.*

"I'll get on my way then. Order up another pot of tea from below, friend, and ask Mrs. Squidge for a few more sausages, will you? I'll be back in a jiffy."

~

Darkness comes. The wizard waits with growing unease. The tea grows cold, and the ferret does not return.

Cajjer continues to whine and Mrs. Squidge groans incessantly.

~

Over in Gyminge, at the southern command immigration post, Vyruss checks his woodlouses, has supper with Major Bubblewick, and also waits.